ISBN 978-1-365-34786-3

Also by Ajay Joseph:

Once A Stranger

It Will Be All Right

If I Left

The Time of Us

Impulse

Special thanks to Sonja, Will, John, and Janice

SLEEPWALKER

AJAY JOSEPH

Chapter 1

I think miracles are wonderful. We spend our lives not knowing that a particular miracle or blessing is in fact the best thing that could ever happen to us. I know that I may never become President or a billionaire or win a gold medal but for what it's worth, I have experienced many miracles in my life.

Daisy and I were eight when we first met. My neighborhood has these movie in the park nights and my family went. And our moms started to talk about something and one thing led to another and Daisy and I became friends.

Daisy would always tie her hair in a bun, wear running shorts, tie a flannel around her hips, and laugh this amazing laugh that made you want to hear it over and over and over. She was in love with life even though it was hard for her.

I am thoroughly convinced that in your life you meet a handful of people you just know you are supposed to be with. Whether as lovers, or as friends; you meet them in the strangest of circumstances and you wonder if it was fate or coincidence or just dumb luck. But it makes you believe in something.

We'd go to the park together and we'd sit on the swings and talk about our lives. We'd go to the convenient store, get candy, get pop, and get sugar drunk. We'd go to the grocery store and get microwavable meals and heat them up and watch movies late into the night. Then we'd make hot chocolate and sit cross legged on her bed and talk about things bigger than us. And when the sun started to rise, we couldn't believe that we stayed up all night talking.

And I loved it.

Everything changed on May 20, 2012 when Daisy's mother died from cancer. Daisy cried and cried for days and it sent her entire family sprawling into sadness. Eventually she got over it but there was always an emptiness in her heart. We had spent so many nights staying up late talking about it.

Daisy oftentimes found her heart getting broken. The two boyfriends she had broken her heart because of all the lying and cheating that went on. Each time it happened, she felt like something was wrong with her. Like she wasn't good enough for them.

"It's like my heartstrings have come undone," she would always say.

"What do you mean?"

"It means I try to be faithful. I will always be there for the ones I care about. But who's going to be there for me? My heart has been broken so many times I'm surprised I'm still capable of loving people. But even at the moment when they come undone, I will stay with you."

That's what made Daisy so different from everyone else. Her heart had room for everyone. She saw the best in everyone and always wanted to be positive. Despite the hardships she went through, love radiated from her. And maybe she loved others so much she forgot to love herself.

Chapter 2

I got to school and parked Becky into the parking lot. Becky was my poor excuse of a car that ran on duct tape, gasoline, and prayer. But she got me where I needed to go and hasn't given up on me yet.

I walked into my school and went straight up to the third floor where my locker was. I opened it, gathered what I needed for my first period Humanities class and then started heading down to class.

"Michael Wilson."

I already knew it was my friend Isaac.

"You, my friend, need to get a new car," he said. Isaac was a little shorter than me with straight black hair and tan skin. He was pretty much a geek but he was my best friend nonetheless.

"When I have about ten thousand dollars then I can get a new car," I said. "Till then, Becky's all we've got."

"I mean I guess. Oh by the way, Melanie and I've been talking."

I tried to remember who this Melanie was.

"The girl from the gas station?"

"Oh right. Her …"

"You totally forgot who she is."

"Yeah."

Isaac sighed sharply. "She's the one who owns the Pontiac? Becky's inferior complex?"

I pointed at his chest. "You don't even *have* a car so you better appreciate Becky for all she does for you."

Isaac pushed my hand away. "All I'm saying is she's an amazing girl and I want to impress her."

"Please tell me you haven't showed her your stupid Hydro Ranger collection."

"I haven't *showed* her anything. I just *told* her about it –"

"That's not any better."

"And she said that it's cute. Cute! Hydro Ranger isn't *cute!* He could zap her pretty face off with one finger."

"Isaac if you really like this girl, please don't be weird around her."

We were walking through the halls until I got to my Humanities class. Isaac had general music first period so that meant he could be late since the teacher was pretty chill. Then I saw Daisy. With Bret.

I'm not sure what my expression was like because Isaac said. "You miss her, don't you?"

"No," I lied.

"You can't lie to me."

"I'm not lying."

"Michael it's okay, man. You and her were really close. You miss her. It's okay."

"And now she's with Bret."

"Yeah," he said slowly. "But the important thing is that you and her have been friends since you were kids. She can't forget that."

"But it seems like she *has* forgotten me."

"Doubt it."

I glanced over and saw Bret kissing Daisy, they broke apart, and he went to class and she was walking down the hallway. At that moment, I wasn't sure if I should look at her or just go to class. But we made quick, awkward eye contact and she smiled. I don't remember if I smiled because the only thing I was thinking was how close we once were and now we were practically strangers.

The bell rang and I walked into Humanities where I took my seat next to my other good friend, Fabian.

"Did you hear about Isaac and Melanie?" he asked.

"That she texted him back?" I asked, taking out my notebook.

"Yeah. He's going to ask her to prom."

"Seriously? They just met."

Fabian shrugged. "Isaac."

I nodded and agreed. "Isaac." That was enough of an explanation.

"Hi, Michael."

I turned to see Kimberly taking her seat in front of my desk. Kimberly and I met this past year and we were pretty cool with each other. She was a great girl who was funny, smart, and pretty with thick curly hair and dark brown eyes.

"What's up, Kimberly Avocado?"

She rolled her eyes at me. "Ex*cuse* me? It's Acevdeo. Not Avocado."

"Are you talkin' to me?" I replied in a New York accent.

"Yeah boy," she replied in the same accent. *"What dey is it todey?"*

"Today is Thursdey, ya filthy slob. Do you have da homewerk?"

Kimberly rummaged through her bag and pulled out her Humanities binder and took out the sheet. *"Bada bing bada boom."*

"Thanks a lawwt."

"You bet."

And then we started laughing because talking in a New York City accent was what we did together. It was always our thing once I found out she was originally from New York City and from then on, it became our thing. Of course neither of us could really *do* a New York City accent but it was fun nonetheless.

The whole part about Kimberly Avocado was because when she first said it, I thought she said avocado but, of course, that wasn't her last name. So naturally, it became a way to tease her.

Mr. Collins walked into the room followed by the Cow. It stood for computers on wheels.

"Okay everyone," Mr. Collins said. "The Cow is here so you have the period to work on your papers."

He began handing them out to us and we turned them on and started to "work."

"Hey, Kimberly? Can I see your laptop?"

She handed it to me and I pressed two keys at the same time that rotated her screen and gave it back to her.

"What did you do?! Fix it!"

I laughed evilly. *"Nooo."*

Kimberly gave me a disgusted look and pressed the same keys a few times and fixed the screen. Then she looked at me, eye brows raised.

"Oh," I said.

"How do you feel?"

"I feel great."

A little while later, Fabian said, "Michael, how are you starting off the paper?" He leaned over to look at my screen to which I began typing *Fabian sucks he is lame and not cool.* "You suck, Michael."

The day wore on.

I am a firm believer in school and learning, but stuffing eight hours of it in one day with each of those classes having at least an hour's worth of homework, give or take the class, there just aren't enough hours in the day. Not to mention other commitments such as sports or work. Plus like I said, I like to learn. School isn't even about learning any more, it's about passing.

Daisy and I would talk about how corrupt our school system is – Van Buren especially.

"I don't even know why they call it school improvement day. I come back to school and the school has not improved."

I sighed as I was walked to and fro class to class. At this point in the year, I was crossed between which college to go to. I was waiting on my acceptance letters to Milton and Kaplan University which were my two choices. So far I hadn't heard anything from either of them and that made me nervous.

At the end of the school day, I was at my locker and the three of us were having an argument.

"Look you don't actually *know* the muffin man," Isaac said.

"He's right, all we know is where he lives," I agreed. "He lives on Drury Lane. But which is his house?"

"Okay he clearly bakes muffins, right? We would just have to go to the bakery and he'd be there," Fabian contested. "Plus if you find the gingerbread man you'd find the muffing man."

"You mean the old man in the gingerbread man story is the muffin man?" I wondered.

"I mean he could be," Fabian said.

"What about the woman?" Isaac wondered.

"Maybe she's the little old lady who lived in the shoe," I offered.

"And the shoe is the muffin man's house. So that's what we have to look for on Drury Lane."

Isaac's eyebrows rose and he said, "Illuminati confirmed."

The three of us started laughing and it felt so good. I love people who can make me laugh.

I closed my locker and the three of us headed down the hall and out of the school. That was when I saw the door open to a classroom and saw Daisy walk out of it.

"Hi," Daisy said in such a quiet voice I didn't remember if she even said anything.

"Hey," I said, just in case.

But she kept on walking and my heart felt sad because that was the first word either of us have spoken to each other in about a year and a half. Almost two years.

Isaac and Fabian didn't say anything about it and I was glad. All I wanted was ice cream.

Chapter 3

"I want to introduce you guys to Melanie," Isaac said once we were in Becky. "I think now's the time."

"Technically *I* introduced *you,* " I reminded him.

"What exactly happened?" Fabian asked.

"We were at the gas station one day," I started. "And this girl at the stall thing next to us was like 'hey do you have any paper towels there?' 'cause I guess she was washing her car or something. And I gave her some and she's like 'thanks.' Then she asked about my car and how sorry it looks and how amazing her car was. Meanwhile, Isaac comes back from inside getting us candy and then those two end up talking because he was surprised she knew about cars."

"You don't think girls can know about cars?" Fabian asked.

"No that's *not* what happened!" Isaac protested. "All I said was 'wow it's so cool you know so much about cars.' And *she* took it the wrong way, thinking I was being sexist. Either way, she gave me her number and we've been talking ever since and I want you guys to meet her. She said to meet her at Sandy's."

"Ugh," I said. "Do we *have* to?"

"Yes. Come on. The groomsmen have to meet the bride."

"Shut up, Isaac."

I pulled into the parking lot at Sandy's and the three of us found a booth and ordered burgers, fries, and shakes. I think after a day like today, I needed comfort food.

"I don't think she's coming," Fabian said. "She blew you off."

"No she's coming," Isaac said convincingly. "Look, there she is now."

We looked out the window and saw a silver Pontiac pull up and park right next to my lemon of a car. I suppose a normal person might have felt self-conscious but I wasn't. Melanie got out of her car and she clicked the doors locked. She was wearing an Aztec patterned romper with her hair tied up in a bun on her head and had on sunglasses. She had a white purse she carried in the crook of her arm and her phone was in the same hand.

"Ain't she *purty,*" Isaac warbled.

"You talk to her like that and she'll smack you," I said.

The door opened and we assumed non assuming positions.

"Melanie!" Isaac called out, waving. She walked closer and he stood up, giving her a hug. Suddenly the entire restaurant seemed to be filled with the aroma of strawberries. Or rain. Whatever. It smelled nice.

"These are my friends," Isaac said, scooting in the booth. "You remember Michael from the gas station?"

"The one with the terrible car," she said. "Yes I remember you."

"Nice to see you again," I said flatly.

"And this is Fabian."

Melanie smiled and so did Fabian.

"So we already ordered so you can too if you're hungry," Isaac told her.

"I'm *always* hungry." Melanie took the menu and started looking through it. "Hmm, I wonder if I get the family sized portion if it can be just for me."

I liked this girl already.

Our waitress came back seeing that we had a new member to our party.

"Could I get the double bacon cheeseburger with medium fries and a large iced tea, please?" she said in one breath.

"Sure thing," Ms. Waitress said. "And your guys' food is coming."

"Thank you," I said.

"So!" Melanie declared. "Tell me about yourselves."

"Well …" Fabian started. "I play baseball."

"Position?"

"Second base."

Melanie nodded. "And what about you, Mr. Lemon of a car?"

"I do a lot at school," I told her. "Clubs and freshman mentor stuff. I also play volleyball."

"Nice, nice, I like it. Yeah I don't know if you guys know, but I graduated high school last year. I went to Millbrooke High."

"So are you in college now?"

She shook her head in disgust. "Oh no! I couldn't go *straight* into twelve more years of education! I needed a break first."

"Twelve years?" Fabian asked.

Melanie nodded. "I plan on being a neurosurgeon."

"Where did his whole desire come from?" I asked.

"Well I spent a lot of time in hospitals as a kid," she said up front.

"Oh …" I said starting to feel sorry for her.

"You think it relates to some sort of disease." She laughed. "No it's not that. My church partnered with a hospital and I volunteer there like every summer and I met a lot of the doctors and I love what they do."

"That's cool," I said. "I have no idea what I want to do as a career."

Melanie shrugged. "You have time to figure it out."

Ms. Waitress came back with our food and we figured out who ordered what and we began to eat.

"Okay Melanie," Isaac said. "We need your opinion on something."

"Hm," she said.

"Hydro Ranger versus Nova."

"Nova for sure."

"Oh my gosh what? Hydro Ranger can literally cause lighting from *anywhere!*"

Melanie laughed at Isaac. "Are you seriously going to compare someone who has power over energy over someone who can cause lightning?"

I wasn't into this comic book stuff like Isaac and Melanie were but I guess Fabian and I were thinking the same thing and we just stayed quiet and let those two talk and bond.

"Plus Hydro Ranger has a huge situational awareness around him," Isaac pointed out. "He can see Nova's attacks from a mile away."

"Not like he could escape them!"

"I don't care. I still like Hydro Ranger. I think he's amazing. Nova is cool too but Hydro Ranger has been my hero since day one."

Melanie shrugged and continued eating her double bacon cheeseburger. I know that I shouldn't have let it get to me, but I remembered all the times Daisy and I would talk about things like this. We hadn't spoken in so long I was starting to forget who she was.

After we were done with our late lunch, Isaac and Melanie went off to the comic book store and I drove Fabian home. I got up to my room, slung my backpack off, and flopped down on my bed and let out a long sigh.

I got up a little while later and turned on my desktop to finish typing a paper for English class. The worst part about there being one month left for school was having so many assignments left to complete.

"Whatcha doing?" my bratty sister Abby said.

"Homework," I said.

She snickered. "You have to do *homework.* I'm *done* with it."

"Wait until you get older, then you'll be doing homework all night long."

"Really?"

"Yes, don't you see how late I stay up?"

"I just thought you always were up all night talking to your girlfriend."

She meant Daisy and I felt another twang of pain my chest. Why did today have to suck so much?

"She's not my girlfriend," I said. "We don't even talk anymore."

"Why not?"

"I don't know. I mean … things change; people change."

"But … you were friends … and I liked her."

That's true. Daisy was Abby's babysitter when Abby was growing up and the two had gotten close. Daisy spun her wit, charm, and humor on Abby and the two had become partners in crime. One time they sabotaged my room by throwing my underwear all over the place. Another time when Abby had scraped her knee, Daisy very gently cleaned her wound and put a bandage over it. Then they went out for ice cream.

"Yeah," I said. "I like her too."

"You *like her* like her?"

"No," I said.

"Yes you *dooo!*"

"Abby, can you like, not?! I have stuff to do."

Abby ran off to her room leaving me in peace and quiet to work. I rubbed my face in my hands and rubbed my eyes. I was never sure if I liked Daisy. I mean it just never really came up I guess. We were just good friends. But was there something more?

I pushed the thoughts away and began working on my paper.

Chapter 4

I am not into parties. My version of a party is getting some friends together at my house, eating pizza, listening to music, watching a movie, and just talking. So parties that have alcohol, wine coolers and all that jazz I am opposed to.

"I mean you don't have to drink," Isaac said during lunch the next day. "Just come and hang out with us. Melanie'll be there."

"Isaac, that doesn't make me want to go," I said.

"Just come. Plus you have a car. If you want to leave, you can just walk out and drive home and be deprived of social interaction and live your life alone."

"Yeah because that's *exactly* what'll happen."

"Okay you can decide if you want to come but Isaac," Fabian said, turning to Isaac. "Melanie's a year older than you. Something must be seriously wrong with her to want to talk to *you.*"

"Something *is* wrong with her because she likes Nova over Hydro Ranger."

"I have to agree with her though. Nova is much stronger than Hydro Ranger."

"Oh not you too!"

Fabian shrugged. "Sorry, man, but the facts prove it."

This whole time I was debating the pros and cons of going to this party. I didn't even know whose party it was. And the question *I* had was will there be food there.

"Oh look who it is," Fabian said.

I looked over and saw Bret and some of the other Lax Bros assembling together, being unnecessarily loud.

"DUDE," one of them said.

"We got them! We the best there is!" another Lax Bro said.

"There ain't nobody that can stop us!" Bret screamed.

There was a girl in their midst and she had a lacrosse stick strapped to her backpack. She was celebrating with them too.

"I don't understand why they're jubilating over winning this game," Isaac said.

"Didn't they lose like *eight* in a row?" I asked.

"They did. And now they won this one game and think they're painting the town red."

"What's up with your words today?"

"My friend, the English language is full of idioms that are fun to use."

I realized it was just Isaac being Isaac so I decided to ignore it. I noticed that there were others in the lunchroom who were smiling at the Lax Bros like they were proud of them.

Out rightly I said, "Our lacrosse teams *sucks*. "Why is everyone getting so hyped over it?"

Fabian nodded. "Right. Why not celebrate a team that's actually good like all our volleyball teams or baseball or track or softball? I don't even understand lacrosse."

"It's like football and soccer and hockey all in one, right?" I wondered. "I don't know. I don't like it."

"Is it because Bret plays it?"

That caught me off guard completely. "No? Why'd you say that?"

"I mean he sorta took Daisy away from you."

"He didn't *take* her away from me. Things change and people change. It's normal."

Fabian shook his head. "Don't try and hide how you truly feel about her. I know you're not jealous of Bret; you're better than that. But we all know that you and her were like two peas in a pod and now she's shooting the breeze with Bret."

"Seriously why are you guys using these weird idioms today?"

"Michael," Isaac said seriously. "Don't try to change the subject. The more you suppress the way you feel about her and this whole situation, the only thing that'll happen is you're gonna feel stronger about it."

Fabian nodded. "It's clear that you have strong feelings for her. If not in a romantic way, then you really care for her as a friend. And that's okay. Tell me: would it be so bad to let her know how much you care? All of *us know*. Would it be so wrong for *her* to know?"

I felt like a sponge soaking up all these emotions. I just didn't want this to be such a big deal. I am thankful that I have people in my life like Isaac and Fabian but … there was something different about Daisy. Maybe it was because we had known each other when we were kids. Maybe it was because we were there for each other during the darkest times in our lives.

Maybe it was because I *did* love her.

"You know what?" I said. "I'm going to that party."

Chapter 5

"Potatoes have skin. I have skin. Therefore I am a potato," Isaac announced.

"You make me want to hit you," Kimberly said from the passenger side while the five of us were piled in Becky. Melanie came along and she wouldn't stop talking smack about my car. ("Michael, this car is pretty awful.")

"It's a simple case of if A equals B and B equals C then A equals C," Isaac explained. "I am a potato."

"Okay Isaac. Fine. You're a potato," I said. I heard him laughing to himself.

I found the party house and parked alongside the street. We got out and walked up to the front door, which was open, and we stepped inside. Music with heavy base was playing and there were a lot of people in this place.

"Hey, girl!" another girl said, walking up to Kimberly.

"Hey!"

She took Kimberly's hand and took her away.

We went into the kitchen where there were drinks all around the counter. And thankfully they had pop so I poured myself a cup of some. Melanie opened a bottle of beer and took a swig of it.

"Now what do we do?" I muttered mostly to myself.

"Now ..." Melanie took a long drink of beer. *"We party!"* She grabbed Isaac's hand and they dashed off together somewhere. That left Fabian and I together. We wandered through the living room where a lot of people from school were and we said hey to them.

Suddenly, some girl named Jasmine slumped into Fabian's arms.

"Isn't this party *ah-mazing?"* Jasmine slurred. She was extra happy and I knew that she was a wee bit tipsy.

"Yes," Fabian said. "It's amazing."

"Faaabian!"

"Very good, Jasmine. You know my name."

Fabian and I looked at each other and were snickering. We both knew Jasmine and when she wasn't like this, she was great.

Jasmine gasped loudly and a look of concern filled her face. She stumbled closer to Fabian and put her hands on his face. "Did you know ... H_2O has *two* parts of oxygen to it? I'm going to be a *doctor!"*

I looked at Fabian and I did not stop myself from laughing. Jasmine turned and gave me a disgusted look but turned back to Fabian with the expression like she just discovered the secret to humanity's origins.

"Oh my gosh Jasmine I did not know that!" Fabian said with mock excitement.

"Isn't it *ah-mazing?"*

"Tell me something I don't know."

"I know that because I'm going to be a doctor!"

By this point, Jasmine put her hands off his face and then hugged him so tightly she would never let go.

"You're always there for me, Fabian," she said.

"Uh huh."

"Don't ever leave me."

"I'm right here."

"Thank you."

Then Jasmine pushed herself away and exclaimed, *"I'm going to be a doctor!"*

"Oh *are* you now?"

Jasmine nodded furiously. "Yes!"

At some point, Jasmine and Fabian went off together and I was by myself. I suddenly started to feel very awkward and out of place. There were a lot of people here and this wasn't the kind of place you'd see me at. It wasn't my crowd.

I made my way back to the kitchen where it was a little more breathable. I poured myself another glass of pop and look a deep breath.

"You alright?"

I turned around and saw Melanie standing there, a bottle in her hand. I suddenly didn't want to talk to her or anyone else for that matter.

"Yeah," I lied. "I'm great."

She didn't look convinced but she dropped it. She went to the fridge and pulled out two bottles and took the caps off them.

"Melanie? Do you really think you should be drinking that much?"

She scoffed. "Learn to live a little, Michael."

She walked back the way she came with the bottles in her hands and I was left by myself, feeling a combination of confusion, loss, and anxiety.

This shouldn't have been hard for me.

"Hey."

It was Daisy.

When I met Kimberly or Melanie or pretty much anyone else for that matter, I could only see them as the seventeen, or nineteen, year old they were. When I looked at Daisy, I saw the eight year old girl who used to play at the park. I saw the eleven year old who told me about the boy she liked. I saw the fourteen year old who came to me crying because of her mother passing away.

And seeing her now just brought back all those memories.

"How've you been?" she asked somewhat cautiously.

"Good," I said. "How are you?"

"I'm alright."

This was terrible. Conversation was never this hard between us.

"That's good," I said. I tried to notice something different about her. "Um …"

"This is pretty awkward, isn't it?" she asked, chuckling.

"Yeah. It really is."

She stepped into the kitchen and sat on one of the bar stools across me. "You know something? I wish this party had ice cream."

"That'd be great. I would love ice cream right now."

"You still like those ones on a stick?"

I nodded. She remembered.

She shook her head and smiled. "I always hated ice cream on a stick."

"'Cause it'd always melt once you touched it," I remembered, a smile creeping on my face. "You always had to have it in a bowl."

"I did! Because that way it wouldn't melt all over my hand."

"And I bet it's still the same way?"

"Of course. Bret gives me crap about it all the time but hey, this is who I am."

"Yeah," I said. My smile slowly faded away.

"Anyway …"

I wanted to say something to her. All I wanted to ask her why we haven't spoken in so long when that's all we did every day when we were growing up. Why did it have to stop? I never wanted it to stop.

"But, um … how are *you* doing? I mean. You know … with …"

"I'm doing okay."

Daisy of all people knew that I was *not* okay but this wasn't the time or place for a conversation like this.

"Maybe I should get back to Bret," she said softly.

"Yeah."

"It was really good to see you, Michael."

"You too, Daisy."

She didn't turn around right away; something in her eyes told me she was tired. Tired of the way her life was playing out. And she wanted someone to be there for her. I had a right to say that because I knew her for so long. She once had a certain glow in her face that wasn't there anymore. Where had it gone?

Then Daisy turned around, her head down, and walked out of the kitchen and I wasn't sure how to feel. I was so happy to have finally talked to her, even if it was just about ice cream and not about our lives. But that's all I wanted. To just sit together on a rooftop somewhere late at night and talk about all the things we've been through.

And then Melanie came back into the kitchen with Isaac and they pulled out more bottles of beer. And I wanted to smack them out of their hands and scream at them. But I restrained myself from doing so.

Instead I walked out of the house and sat in Becky and leaned my head against the steering wheel and I sighed heavily. Thankfully no one was around to see me. What I really wanted was for someone to be with me. I was not expecting the night to turn out like this but now that it had, I had to deal with it.

Right then and there, Becky seemed to be my only friend.

"Becky," I said "I'm sorry for saying you're a stupid car."

And then I leaned my head on the headrest and tried to control my breathing.

At some point, the others came out of the house and all got into my car.

"You *okayyy, broo?"* Fabian asked.

"Yeah," I said, rubbing my eyes and sniffing. "I'm good.

"Are you *baked, bro?"* Isaac asked from the back seat. "Your eyes are red ... like a tiger."

"No I'm fi –"

"Wait a minute!" Melanie interjected. "Isaac? Tigers are *orange!"*

Isaac gasped so dramatically. "No. *Way ..."*

"Michael?" Melanie continued. "Why don't you turn on this rust bucket of a car and drive?"

I gripped the steering wheel until my knuckles turned white. I whirled around and glared at her. "You know something, Melanie? If you don't like this car, you can get out right now and find your own way home! I am sick and tired of you always having to say something it. If it's such a problem, you can drive your car around and never have to sit here ever again."

There was silence in the car. I knew that maybe I shouldn't have snapped at her but I didn't really care at the moment. I was too overwhelmed with everything else.

No one said anything so I started to drive. I dropped everyone off one by one and made sure they got inside their house before driving off.

When I dropped Isaac off, Fabian was left and he must have sobered up a little bit because he asked, "What was up with you snapping at Melanie?"

I leaned my head against my headrest and sighed. "I don't know, man. I just ... I got angry."

"What for?"

"A lot of things. I talked to Daisy. It wasn't anything, just about what kind of ice cream we like. Then she asked if I was okay because of what happened to Malachi and that was pretty much it. Then I walked out of the party and sat inside here and ..."

I knew I just put a huge damper on everyone's night.

"Dude, I know it's been rough on you since what happened to Malachi last month," he said slowly. "But you can't let something like that affect everything you do and who you become. I mean … you know that bad things happen and there may be nothing you can do about it, but you have to learn from those moments."

"I know," I said truthfully. I put the car in gear and drove Fabian home. We were silent the entire way. Once we got to his house, he said, "Call me if you need anything."

I drove back to my house and parked on the street. I walked into my house and my mom was in the kitchen with Abby and they were baking cookies.

"Hi, Michael," my mom said. She took one look at me and concern filled her face. "What's wrong?"

I shook my head. "Nothing; just tired."

I headed straight for my room and grabbed my towel. I took a long, hot shower and then walked back to my room where I fell on my bed, put my headphones in my ears and blasted music, wanting to drown out this entire day.

Chapter 6

The next few days were relatively boring. Nothing much happened at school or at home. We didn't discuss what happened after the party when I snapped at Melanie nor did Fabian and I talk about how I was feeling. I just tried not to think about the whole thing.

About four days later, at lunch, Isaac had some news for us.

"I am no longer talking with Melanie," he said.

"What? Why not?" Fabian asked.

He quickly glanced at me. "I realized that she and I just weren't compatible."

Kimberly rolled her eyes. "Why don't you tell us what *really* happened?"

"Well … okay fine. A few days after the party, she and I were talking and she's saying how she *hates* Michael and that he had no right to yell at her like that."

"I mean honestly she deserved it," Kimberly said. "She was being rude to him."

I shrugged. "I couldn't care less about her but continue."

"So then I try to tell her that it *was* rude of her to criticize his car and she tries to defend herself because she was drunk at the time so she didn't know what she was saying so I reminded her of all the other times she talked about your car."

"This Becky of yours is causing quite the drama," Fabian teased.

"So then the conversation turns into whose side *I'm* on," Isaac continued. "At this point, I was getting real tired of this woman because she's being unnecessarily complicated and quite annoying to say the least. So then I just say 'Melanie Vo, you are undoubtedly an amazing creature but one that lacks basic human decency and social decorum for regards when it comes to other people's emotions and for that, I wish to never see you again.'"

"You said exactly that?" Fabian asked.

Isaac nodded. "Something like that."

"Well I'm glad no other girls are in this group," Kimberly said, sitting back in her chair, content with the situation. "Although there seems to be so much drama with the three of you here."

To which Isaac replied, "This, Kimberly, is caused by a pheromone we emit that repels members of the opposite sex when the interaction in question is one of romance thus causing said drama."

"You know what I think is stupid?" Kimberly began.

Here we go.

"Like how these high school boyfriends and girlfriends get matching tattoos. Like … *seriously?* I mean I guess at least one part of the relationship will last forever."

"Kimberly, do *you* have an embarrassing tattoo you want to tell us about?" Fabian said.

"No! I plan on staying *single*. And if I ever *do* get a tattoo it'll be my sister's name here." She ran her finger alongside of her ribs.

"What's her name?"

"Jacqueline but we call her Jackie."

"Nah man with this whole Melanie thing, I learned something," Isaac said randomly. "You wanna know how to get a girlfriend?" You just go up to a girl and be like 'aye, girl, you my girlfriend for the next two months.' Then when the two months are up, you go 'alright, I'm out.' Then you're a free agent."

We started to laugh and once again, it felt good. For that brief moment, nothing else mattered but me and my friends and laughing together. It actually was very healing since my thoughts were a sickness that laughter seemed to be the only cure for.

Chapter 7

That weekend, Daisy Vargas, rang my doorbell.

"Hi," she said awkwardly. She was wearing jean shorts, a white T-shirt, on it was a hand with an eye on it, and had a black hoodie tied around her waist with her hair in a bun and sunglasses on her head.

"Hey," I said. At one point, I didn't need to say anything more and Daisy would walk right in the house but now it was like I was talking to a girl scout trying to sell cookies.

"Um, are you busy today?"

"No," I said. "I already finished my homework so I'm not doing anything."

"Cool." A beat. "I mean me neither 'cause I too finished my homework."

"Yeah …"

"And it's such a nice day today."

After a pause I could tell Daisy was about to grit her teeth and ask whatever she wanted to. She always got this worried look for about a split second and then narrowed her eyes. Her lips would quiver as she spoke but you wouldn't know she was nervous because her entire face showed otherwise.

"Youwannagogeticecream?" she asked.

I understood. "I'd love to." Another beat. "Just let me get my wallet. Um …"

"I can wait out here."

"Nonono come on in."

I stepped back and opened the door wider for her. She stepped inside and she seemed to get smaller. I noticed she was looking around but she was trying to be subtle about the whole thing.

Oh what the heck.

"We haven't changed the place around a lot," I said.

"Yeah it's just like I remembered it."

Once you walked inside, the living room was to the right and two couches sat adjacent to each other in front of a coffee table and other chairs surrounding it. To the right of the couch was a TV. The left side was the dining room with a mahogany table and a small chandelier above it.

"Remember how we'd come home from school and sit around here and watch TV and *not* do homework?" she asked suddenly.

Just go with it, I told myself.

"I remember. Sophomore year especially because of geometry class. Ms. Mayer was a *terrible* teacher!"

"Ms. Mayer was amazing! Geometry wasn't that bad. But chemistry?"

"Chemistry was easy. Plus you had Mr. Basa; he literally gave you the answers for each test and let you use it on the test."

"You don't understand, Michael. I second guess myself so much I start to doubt my own notes."

I shrugged. "Good thing we had each other for tutoring."

"You were a lost cause for geometry though," Daisy said with a smirk and that's how I knew she was back.

"I will *forever* struggle with math. I feel like I have dyslexia but with numbers."

"I think sophomore year was just a really dumb year in general."

Daisy and I laughed for a second and then Abby came into the room. She even took a step back once she saw Daisy.

"Hi, Abby," Daisy said, her eyes glowing. The last time she saw Abby was when she was nine. Now almost a year and a half later, Abby had gotten taller.

"Hi," Abby said strangely.

"It's good to see you."

"Yeah …"

Noticing that this was going to get awkward much faster than it needed to, I said, "Daisy and I are going to get some ice cream."

"Okayy," Abby said.

"Tell mom, okay?"

Abby nodded.

Daisy and I went to my bedroom and on the way up there, I realized how messy it was. Before I didn't care but now I was very self-conscious about how messy it was and if it smelled.

"Are those your trophies from volleyball?" she asked.

She was talking about our teams back-to-back city championship titles we won last year and this past one. Not to mention our JV team won back-to-back titles as well. But lacrosse got all the attention. I had a trophy for MVP from this past season and the Coach's Award last season. Plus a few medals from winning a few games here and there.

And for the record, our lacrosse team hasn't won jack.

"Yeah," I said.

"I watched you play."

"Really?"

I knew people from our school came out and watched us play; it just never crossed my mind that maybe Daisy came to watch.

"I came to all your home games."

"Oh wow. Thank you."

She nodded. "You have a killer spike."

I smiled. "Thanks. I love spiking."

She smiled. Why was this so awkward?

I grabbed my wallet and walked down the stairs and out the door. Daisy insisted we walk instead of drive and I was all for it. It *was* such a nice day after all.

"How are Isaac and Fabian?" she asked.

"They're good," I said. "Actually Isaac was getting involved with a girl who'll be a sophomore in college but long-story-short, they're not talking anymore."

"What happened? How'd they meet?"

"Well we met at a gas station when she needed paper towels and then Isaac and her started talking. Then he introduced us to her and she was kinda cool. Then we went to the party where she got, like, *drunk* and I basically yelled at her because she always had to talk about my car and how it sucks."

"Good," Daisy said. "She sounds like a jerk."

"Yeah she kinda is."

"Why'd you yell at her?"

"I didn't *yell* yell at her; just sort of said it firmly. I was just getting emotional at the party because I saw so many people drinking and it reminded me of Malachi."

A hush came between us.

"Sorry," I said. "I didn't mean to damper the mood."

"No you're fine. How are you, by the way? I asked you at the party but it wasn't the right time."

"Alright, I guess. It's hard to believe he's gone because of something like that but ..."

"But what?"

"But nothing. It happened. No use dwelling on the past."

"I know you were so there for me when my mom died," Daisy said. She was looking down and her voice was quiet. "I'm sorry I haven't there for you when your brother died."

I waved my hand in the air, dismissing the subject. "Don't worry about it. Things happen and we can't *always* be there for each other."

"But you? Freshman year when it happened, I mean we were starting school, you were getting into volleyball and were doing so good at it. Not to mention school. You *made* time."

I didn't, was what she was saying.

"Maybe because I didn't want you to be alone."

When we got to the ice cream parlor, we ordered ice cream and sure enough, Daisy had to have it in a bowl.

"Don't judge me, Michael," she said firmly.

"No judgment here," I assured her.

We went outside and sat in front of each other, eating our ice cream. It was so hard to believe that after about a year we were back together like old times.

"Michael … we're friends, right?" she asked.

I don't know, I thought. It had been *such* a long time since we last talked and things were awkward between us. Three months before junior year ended, we had lost contact and all this time later, here we were.

And the worst part about it all was that maybe in between that whole time, I might have started to get feelings

44

for her. Not necessarily in a romantic way but feelings to make sure that she was okay.

"We're friends," I said reassuringly. "But it's been so long since we've actually *been* friends."

She looked down and said, "It's been hard."

"What do you mean?"

"After my mom died, it started a terrible revolution in my family. My dad? He started drinking, starting staying out late. He remarried and now I have a little step brother."

During late sophomore year and early junior year, it was difficult to get time to be together because of the downward spiral in her family. Today was the first time we were really getting to talk about it.

"It's been pretty hard," she said. I suddenly realized how tired she sounded. Physically, emotionally, and mentally.

"I'm sorry to hear that," I said dumbly.

"It's not your fault."

"I wish there was something I could do."

And then her eyes lit up.

"There *is*. Remember when we were sixteen and you got your license and we took those midnight drives? Do you remember all of our nighttime adventures?"

I smiled as I thought back to those memories.

"Of course I do."

"Remember when we drove to Wisconsin?! We were bored and thought that'd be a good idea?"

I remembered how that was our last late night adventure before we stopped talking.

"That was the best night out *ever.*"

We traded memories on how we went to the park and played on the swings. Or how we'd go to the grocery store and buy microwavable meals and heat them together and watch movies. And the times we drove out anywhere just so we could forget our lives.

"Let's take a midnight drive. Tonight."

I didn't even need to think about my answer. "I'm down," I said. "Just like old times?"

"Just like old times. Live by the sun, love by the moon."

Daisy's face was one of pure happiness and it made me want to see that expression all the time.

Chapter 8

That night I did what I always did when Daisy and I used to sneak out: I went down to the kitchen and pretended to get something to eat when in actuality, I was just waiting for a good time to leave.

Years of living with my parents has taught me that every night at one in the morning, my dad has to use the bathroom. So while he was in there, my mom and Abby were fast asleep, that's when I'd make my escape.

So at one o' clock when I heard my dad's footsteps upstairs, I slipped through the door and quickly locked it and headed to Becky. This was the most dangerous part because whenever I ignite the engine, Becky makes this horrible coughing and sputtering noise that can wake up the entire neighborhood. And if my parents found out what I was doing, then I'd die

"Becky, come on girl," I said soothingly as I sat in. "Please don't be so loud."

I turned the engine on, closed my eyes, and gritted my teeth as Becky began hacking away. I quickly reversed out of the lot and waited in the middle of the street where Daisy was waiting. I noticed she was carrying a bag over her shoulder.

"Hi," she said.

"Hey."

She got in and sat down. Her hair was in a bun on her head and she was wearing running shorts, with a black hoodie wrapped around her hips, a white t shirt, and green flip flops. She looked like the old Daisy I knew from years back.

"Where do you wanna go?" I asked, already starting to drive.

"You know where Horner Park is?" she asked.

"Yeah."

"Let's go there."

Daisy took the AUX cord and plugged her phone in it and started playing the song we always played to when we ran off in the night.

"I haven't listened to this song in so long," I said.

"I haven't either. It's been *too* long."

"It really has."

"But I'm glad we're here."

"Me too."

"I'm going to play this song on repeat."

I continued driving; Daisy put her window down and was leaning her chin on her arm on the window ledge. It was a nice night.

Eventually we got to Horner Park and Daisy turned off the music. The park was pretty dark except for a few floodlights that were on.

"Come on," she said.

I followed her through the dark and up the hill where once we were at the top, Daisy took out a blanket from her bag and we spread it on the ground. Then she took off her flip flops and sat down on it. I was wearing athletic sandals and I took them off and joined her on the blanket. She laid down and I sat with my arms behind me.

"Daisy, can I ask you a question?" I said.

"Hm."

"Why did we stop talking?"

And then I was starting to think that might not have been the right thing to say.

"Sorry," I added quickly.

"No it's okay," she said. "I've been wondering the same thing too."

"Why do you think so?"

And then she thought for a while.

"Probably because things changed for me. And for you too. I started dating Bret and we spent more time together. I have my baby brother to take care of now 'cause my dad certainly isn't going to."

"You could have reached out to me," I said. "I was always your friend."

"I know, Michael. I know. I just … I didn't know anything anymore. I see bruises on my step mom all the time and I hate it. We are struggling financially so hard the only place we can go shopping is the thrift store."

I felt so bad for her. How could the girl who was so in love watch helplessly as her own life deteriorated?

"I just feel *stuck*," she continued. "Like I'm going nowhere."

I wasn't sure what to say to her. There was a time when if she was feeling down, all I'd need to do is put my arm around her and that'd be it. She'd lean into my shoulder and we'd be alright in the end.

Suddenly Daisy sat up and started digging through her bag. She pulled out a capsule of pills.

"Medicine?" I asked. "What's it for?"

Daisy looked at the pills and then stuffed them back in her bag. "They're for my depression."

"Oh ..." I said. *She has depression?* How much *had* happened since we last talked?

"But I refuse to take these pills," she said. "I am quite capable of curing my depression on my own. It's all a matter of perspective."

And then I did something I wasn't sure if it was right: I smiled at her.

"What are you smiling for?" she asked.

"Because you're crazy."

"Well ... you're not wrong."

"No not because of the pills. You are a crazy person, Daisy Vargas, and I love that about you. You don't let anyone or anything bring you down. And you are crazy."

She looked at me with an expression I couldn't quite give a name to. But I knew she needed to hear that.

"Michael, I missed you," was all she said. And that was okay because I missed her too. But now we were friends again and it all was going to be alright in the end.

She laid back down and I did too.

"Remember when you said your heartstrings came undone?" I asked.

"Yeah."

"When Malachi died last month, my heartstrings came undone, and right now, it seems like your heartstrings have come undone, so I will stay with you."

"I haven't done a very good job being there for you when yours came undone," she replied.

"It's okay. You were going through your own problems."

"That's no excuse. You were there for me; I can't call myself your friend if I'm not willing to do the same."

It's funny to think that the moments you're experiencing will become memories. Sometimes we don't realize the value of a moment until it *becomes* a memory. So I lay there with her, looking up at the night sky at the beauty and mystery of it all.

And in that moment I knew we were timeless.

Chapter 9

"I need to go back to the motherland like *now,*" Kimberly said firmly during lunch on Monday.

"I too want to go to Mexico," Isaac said. "And Puerto Rico. You're both, right?"

"Yes. But I've been to Puerto Rico before."

"My parents went to Punta Cana last year for a honeymoon," Fabian said.

"I thought you said they went to Mexico," Isaac said.

"I did."

"Punta Cana is in the Dominican Republic."

"No. It's in Mexico."

"What are you talking about? It's in the Dominican Republic, my aunt and uncle went there this past spring."

"No it's not. It's in Mexico.

"Isaac, are you dumb or are you stupid? Punta Cana is in Mexico."

"Are you on *drugs?!*"

"Oh my gosh."

Isaac took out his phone and typed fiercely on it. "I'm looking at the stupid map and it shows Punta Cana right here in the Dominican Republic."

"What Dominica Republic are *you* talking about?"

"The one next to Haiti!"

"Punta Cana is in Mexico!"

"Well it's not showing up on the map is it?!"

"This is so funny," Kimberly said to me and I nodded. "Guys, Punta Cana is a resort in the D.R."

"Oh," Isaac said.

"Seriously?" Fabian asked.

"Uh *yeah.*"

"Oh ..."

"Then where did my parents go?"

"Punta Mita?" Kimberly offered.

"OH!" Fabian exclaimed.

"I guess that clarifies that," Isaac said.

"Guys, can I tell you something?" I asked.

"What's up?" Fabian asked.

"So Daisy and I hung out on Saturday."

"Really? After all this time?"

I nodded. "She came to my house and we went out for ice cream and then we had one of our midnight drives to the park. We just talked about life and now she suffers from depression and has to take medicine but she's not taking it."

"Oh man," Fabian said. "What else?"

"I mean just that her dad remarried, he isn't around anymore, and has a baby step brother to take care of."

"Wow that sounds rough."

"She is going through a lot right now and I just think she deserves better than this."

There was silence for a little bit and then Kimberly said, "Alright, guys, it's been swell but I have to skedaddle. I have to talk with Mr. Banner about my art project."

"Okay," I said. "Bye."

"Bye!"

She took her bag and walked out of the lunchroom.

"She likes you," Isaac said.

I whirled my head at him. "Excuse me?"

"She likes you."

"Not even."

"She *does,*" Fabian said. "Well I don't know about *like* but at the party? She told me that she thinks you're amazing."

"She was probably tipsy or something."

"No she was pretty sober."

"Oh my gosh she does *not* like me."

Isaac and Fabian shrugged. "Okay," Fabian said. "I mean I never seen you do that New York accent with anyone else but her."

"That's 'cause it's our thing we do as a joke. It's our inside joke."

"That's actually an interesting point," Isaac said. "Because if you like a girl and you've got those inside jokes, you have absolutely *zero* chance of dating her. You're friendzoned so hard if you got them inside jokes."

"I don't *like* her, though."

"Okay, okay *fine*. Sorry."

The bell rang soon after and we parted ways.

Kimberly? Likes me?

Nah.

Chapter 10

"I am *never* getting into college."

"You *will,* Michael," my dad reassured me. "Your letter just hasn't come in the mail yet."

"It's never going to."

"If you think negative then only negative will come your way," my mom said.

"Thanks, mom. That makes me feel a lot better."

"Just trying to tell you the truth, Mikey."

"Don't *call* me Mikey."

Later that night, I laid awake in bed just thinking about life and all of its mysteries. I guess I didn't realize how late it was because I must have dozed off. And a rock thrown at my window woke me up. I looked out of it and saw …

Daisy?

I opened my window and there she was standing there bold as brass.

"It's the middle of the night," I whispered.

"I know," she said. "I couldn't sleep. Wanna go out?"

"Out? But … it's a school night."

"And?"

And what the heck?

"Okay, I'll be out soon."

I shut the window, grabbed my windbreaker, put it on, grabbed my keys, and walked downstairs. And in one swift motion, I opened the door and walked outside, shutting it behind me.

"You couldn't have like *called* me?" I asked her.

"Sorry," she said.

"Next time, just text me or something. I think I lost your number when I got a new phone. What was it again?"

"Um ... I don't have a phone anymore. It will have to be my house phone number. And please *don't* call. My dad will flip out."

And then I thought about it for a second. "You know what? Screw phones. I want to get your attention by throwing rocks at your window."

Daisy smiled weakly and we got into Becky.

"Where are we going tonight?" I asked.

"You pick. I chose last time."

"What about that place?"

"Oh *yeah! THAT* one place."

"No, I'm talking about that cliff."

"Brisbane Cliff?"

"Yeah. It's pretty nice up there."

She shrugged. "I'm down."

I started driving and we started playing music. We were off on another nighttime adventure.

"Okay so you know what? I have a hedgehog."

"A hedgehog?" I asked. "What's his name?"

"His name is Hercules but I call him Kuss-Kuss."

"That's adorable."

"I know! He's so cute! I love him so much."

"You always wanted a hedgehog, right?"

"I did. You know the greatest part? He has a girl-friend because my friend also has a hedgehog and it's a girl and she sniffed his butthole so they're dating now. Her name is Bonnie."

I laughed because how cheery she was.

"That's awesome. How long have they been dating?"

"About a year now."

"Wow. Animals have longer relationships with each other than most humans nowadays."

"I'm telling you."

I drove up a winding road and got to Brisbane Cliff where I parked. We stayed in the car and I turned it off. Outside we could see the entire neighborhood and it was very pretty. We were far away enough to see some stars in the sky and I loved it.

"So what's on your mind?" Daisy asked.

"My mind? I don't know … I haven't gotten into Milton University yet."

"Oh that's okay I'm sure you'll get in. They're probably so stunned with your application they're like 'oh my gosh how much money do we give this kid?'"

I smiled at her attempt to make me feel better. "Thanks but I kinda wish they'd let me know. What about you? Did you get into Rockford?"

"Not yet."

I sighed and leaned my head against the headrest.

"You know something?" she said.

"What?"

"I can never see myself doing this with Bret."

Oh man.

"So are you two dating …?"

"We're just talking."

I didn't say anything because I wasn't sure what to say.

"I just feel *stuck.*"

She told me that the night we went to Horner Park.

"Why do you feel that way?"

"I don't know. I feel like … I struggle with little things. I struggle to eat in public. I sometimes get so scared to present in class. It's so hard to get out of bed in the morning to go to school. I mean … I'm scared to ask for *stupid extra napkins* whenever I go out to eat!"

"Daisy," I said slowly. "I know it's hard –"

"No, you wouldn't understand, Michael. I know you're trying to be a good friend right now. But you wouldn't understand this."

I sighed heavily. "You know you're right. I may not know what you're going through but I know what it's like to hurt."

"You want to know what this feels like? It's like a lazy Sunday afternoon manifesting itself for days on end. It feels like I have no control of what's going on and nobody seems to care – there's no way out. And the worst part? You're alone in all of this."

She ran her fingers through her hair and sighed heavily. Her body started to tremble and I could tell she was about to cry. Instinct kicked in and I put my arm around her and she leaned into me. She sobbed silently as I held her.

"Sorry," she said.

"Don't be," I told her. "You're going to make so many friends and you're going to fall in love and you're going to do so many great things."

Then we sat there for a little while, in silence. I was still holding onto her.

"On a lighter note," she said. "I wanted to invite you to come bowling with Bret and I."

"Oh," I said. "Yeah. I'd love to."

"You can bring Isaac and Fabian if you want to also. It'll be a fun friend adventure."

"That sounds great. Could I bring Kimberly too?"

"Who's Kimberly?"

"A friend of mine."

"Oh … yeah sure she can come."

"Great."

"Alright well it's almost one in the morning now."

"Yeah time to head back."

I drove back to our neighborhood and parked the car in my driveway. Daisy and I hugged before she crossed the street to get inside her house. Before she went inside, she looked back at me.

I realized Daisy was the best kind of person there was in the world. The kind of person to help you see the sun where there were clouds. The kind of person who believes in you so much you start to believe in yourself.

We don't usually know when a miracle is taking place in our lives. But I knew meeting Daisy was my miracle.

Chapter 11

"Hey, I'm walkin' here," Kimberly said in our famous New York accent while we were in line in the cafeteria.

"Get outta da way," I retorted.

"Oh hey by the way? Can you read my essay for Humanities?"

"Yeah sure."

"Okay we'll eat first and then go to the library."

"Sounds like a plan."

When we got to our table, Isaac and Fabian were going at it again.

"Bruh, if you use your towel after a shower, how does it get dirty?"

Fabian opened his mouth, about to answer, but he shut up and put his hand over his mouth.

"I mean 'cause it's wet," I said. "But like ... oh my gosh this is a good question."

"Plus, *if* we evolved from monkeys how come we still *have* monkeys?"

"Oh my ... wow," Fabian said.

"These are very important questions, Isaac," Kimberly said, mixing her dressing with her salad.

My eyes were closing and my head was dropping, but I forced myself to stay awake even though falling asleep sounded really good.

"But anyway back to what we were talking about," Fabian said. "The *s* is silent in scent."

"No, the *c* is silent."

"The *s* is."

"How is the *first letter* of a word going to be silent?"

"HAVE YOU EVER HEARD OF A PTERODAC-TAL?"

"Oh … you right."

After we were done eating, Kimberly and I went to the library and we pulled up her essay on one of the computers and I started to read.

"Okay first off," I began. "I think you should take out that last sentence. I don't really see how it relates to the topic."

"What even *is* the topic?" she muttered as she high-lighted the sentence and erased it. I had also just noticed how close I was sitting to her; I could smell her perfume. It smelled like rain. Or strawberries or something. Whatever. Point is: she smelled nice.

The paper wasn't even that long and I finished it quickly and thought it was great.

"Thanks a lawt," she said, putting a hand on my shoulder and letting it fall off. She got up to get it from the printer and returned.

Ask her about bowling with Daisy and Bret.

"Hey so … Daisy and I went for another drive last night," I said awkwardly.

"Really? Is that why you look so tired?"

"I guess so."

"Where'd you go?"

"Brisbane Cliff."

"I love it up there."

"Yeah so anyway … she invited me to go bowling with her and Bret and I was wondering if you wanted to come along." She pursed her lips. "Isaac and Fabian are coming too." I hadn't yet asked them but I was going to make them come.

"That sounds fun," she said. "I'll text you and let you know." When she said *you,* she poked my shoulder.

"Cool."

"So … what'd you guys talk about?"

"Stuff. Some personal stuff about her."

She nodded and didn't press for details, which I liked.

"You know something I noticed?" she said.

"What's that?"

"I've been meaning to tell you this but I wanted to tell you one-on-one. I have a mutual friend with Bret, Landon, and he tells me the only reason he's with Daisy is because he *knows* she'll stay with him."

"What do you mean?"

"Okay look, we all know Daisy's a little shy."

64

Debatable, I thought.

"So maybe the only attention she got from any guy is from Bret. And the only reason Bret is with Daisy is because she's a quiet girl and knows that he's in charge."

I understood what she was trying to say but a part of me didn't want to accept it.

"I mean, you tell me, Michael. Has Daisy had many relationships?"

"She's had a *few,*" I said. "Nothing serious. Just little flings here and there."

"And how did they all end?"

"Well she only had two and they both went badly. She got her heart broken each time. One cheated on her and one got *bored* and left."

"That's why she's going after Bret. He pays attention to her 'cause he's curious about what a quiet girl is like as opposed to the others he's been with."

I hated that. Daisy wasn't just some experiment to run with and see what happens. She was a beautiful person with real feelings.

Thankfully Kimberly kept talking since I had no clue what to say. "If I were you, I'd try to talk to her about this."

"I'm not sure what to talk about," I said truthfully.

"I mean … just try and see how she feels about him. How she *really* feels about him."

I nodded. I probably never would have thought about it that way if it weren't for Kimberly.

The bell rang and we got up to go to our next class.

"Wait," she said. I turned to face her. "Hug."

Then we hugged and after that we let go.

Chapter 12

We agreed to go bowling Saturday afternoon and sure enough, Isaac and Fabian said they'd come.

"Okay guys, real talk," I said.

"Ready," Isaac said.

"I think Kimberly was flirting with me when we were in the library."

"How so?"

"I mean she was touching my shoulder."

"She likes you. She wants *yo number.*"

"She *has* my number. But seriously."

"Try not to think about it too much," Fabian advised. "It probably means nothing."

"It means she's into him."

"Okay look: we'll see how it goes today. If she's acting all flirty then she *may* like me. Not that it's a big deal."

"Do you like her?" Fabian asked.

"Uh … no."

"You hesitated," Isaac pointed out.

"I did not."

"Did so."

"Shut up, Isaac."

Eventually I got to Kimberly's house and we all went to the bowling alley where Bret and Daisy were waiting. Seeing them both together in a non-school setting kind of solidified how they were together. If not dating, at least talking.

"Hey," Daisy said, all smiles. You'd never have known she was crying a few days ago.

We got to the booth and everyone pitched in a few dollars for two lanes, three people each.

"Bret, Michael, and I on one team," Daisy decided. "Isaac, Fabian, and Kimberly on another."

"We about to destroy y'all," Isaac said, sitting at the booth, typing in their names. "Let's all give ourselves nicknames."

"Call me Fab Fabian," Fabian said.

"Nah I'm calling you *Lame.*"

Bret, Daisy, and I simply typed in our normal names and got our bowling balls and waited to start.

"Isaac you should type in your name as *I Suck,*" Kimberly said and I couldn't help but stifle a laugh.

The three of us were lacing up our bowling shoes in silence.

"If I do that, then I'm putting you down as Kimmy."

"Do. Not. *EVER.* Call. Me. *That!*"

"Oh my gosh okay sorry."

I sat there quietly and I couldn't help but wonder how boring it could be three feet away from people who were having a great time.

"Alright," Bret said. "Michael, you're up."

I carried my ball and got to the lane and all ten pins were set up. I bowled and knocked down four out of the ten.

"Nice," Daisy said.

I got the ball again and knocked down three more on my second attempt.

"Kimberly, you suck!"

I turned to see Kimberly's ball rolling down the gutter lane and she was laughing hard.

"Do you want the railings up?" Fabian asked.

"No!" she cried as she walked back to her seat.

It was Fabian's turn and he bowled a strike on the first try.

"Oh okay, *Fabian,*" Kimberly said, flicking her hands at him. "I see you."

I wondered why we weren't having fun on our end.

"Daisy, I swear if you roll a gutter ball …" I said, trying to add some excitement to our lane.

Smirking, Daisy picked up her ball, bowled it, and knocked down seven. She turned back and raised her eye brow.

"Bet you can't get a spare, though."

"Bet."

She bowled a spare.

"We're on the same team here," I pointed out.

We kept on bowling and things weren't as awkward, as such. The others seemed to be having more fun than I was and I started to get pretty bummed since neither Daisy nor Bret wanted to talk really. So then I started talking with Isaac and the others.

"You know what I don't understand?" Isaac asked.

"Everything," Fabian muttered.

Isaac ignored him. "Parking on college campuses. 'Cause I'm already paying tuition, plus room and board, and *on top* of all that, I have to pay to park?"

"Colleges are basically corporations," Kimberly said. "They want as much of your money as they can get."

"But what about education?" Fabian said. "You're getting an education so it's worth the money."

"Yeah but education is a privilege," I said. "Not *everyone* can afford that much."

"Plus college isn't for everyone, in terms of education," Isaac pointed out.

"That's right," Kimberly said. "My cousin didn't finish college and now he owns a small business and he's doing well."

"Well not everyone can be like that if they don't graduate," said Fabian. "Some struggle so much without a degree. And that's what you need in today's world to even have a *shot* at making it."

"Yeah because back in the day if you had a high school diploma, you could get a job," I added. "Now you need a degree and maybe even a masters."

Did you get the whole purpose of the conversation? It wasn't so much about discussing college and money, but it was the four of us talking and Bret and Daisy weren't. They weren't even talking amongst themselves.

It made me wonder whether or not they *really* wanted to be together.

At the end of the game, the others won, only because of Fabian.

"I want a re-match," I said, jokingly.

"You're just sorry that you all lost," Fabian taunted.

"This was only a game," Bret sneered – which surprised all of us because that was probably the first time he spoke today. "I play lacrosse.

Isaac snorted. "It's not like you win in that either." He said that quietly, but loud enough for us to hear, and was looking in the opposite direction.

"Yeah? What do *you* do?"

"I play volleyball; we won back to back city championships."

Bret didn't have anything to say to that and I was glad Isaac said something to shut up that festering ego of his.

To sum up the rest of the day for you: we ate pizza and the four of us were talking the most. Bret and Daisy were awkwardly silent.

"You know, Michael," Kimberly said. "If I was you, I'd want to be me too."

"You're not cool, Kimberly *Avocado!*" I said to her and she was smiling at me.

"Yes I am, Michael," she insisted. "You're just jealous you can't be as cool as me. And this soup is pretty bland. Kimberly took the salt and poured it in her soup. I was just waiting for the opportunity.

"All these flavors and you choose to be salty," I said.

"OH!" Isaac and Fabian went. I even caught a glimpse of Daisy grinning.

Kimberly, looking defeated, was trying to hide a smile.

I looked at Isaac. "Hey, Isaac? You know who's not cool? Kimberly."

"OH!" Isaac cried. "Hey, Kimberly? What's that thing above your neck?"

"My … face? Oh you suck. I hate you all."

We all started laughing and we were having a good time.

"You know when they ask for a parent's signature, you know what I put?" Daisy asked once we were done with pizza.

"What?" I asked.

"The streets."

That got us all laughing. And by all I mean everyone but Bret.

"So you think you're funny?" Isaac challenged.

Daisy smirked. "I *am* funny."

Bret looked annoyed and sighed heavily. I wondered what this problem was.

"Daisy, can I talk to you?" he asked.

Silence followed and Daisy said, "Yeah." They got up and went to a different table and started talking.

"What do you think the problem is?" I whispered to the others.

Kimberly shrugged. "I don't know. I mean … I don't think something happened?"

"Maybe they had a fight last night or something and he decided now was a good time to talk about it," Isaac suggested.

I glanced over at them and saw Daisy giving him a challenging look and he was glaring at her. I wanted to march over there and shut Bret up and take Daisy back with me.

"I hope he treats her good," Kimberly said. "He looks like the kind of guy who'd be stupid."

Suddenly, Bret stood up and he left the pizza parlor. Daisy, too, stood up and walked over to us. She looked a mixture of abandoned and happy.

"What happened?" I asked.

"We just had a little fight," she said. "He said he didn't even want you all to come for this outing but I thought it'd be more fun so he agreed but now that he's here, he hated it."

"Well what the heck, Bret," Isaac said. "No one said you *had* to come."

"That's what I told him. But he said he'd come with me regardless."

"What does that even *mean?*" said Kimberly. "You can't go out on your own?"

Daisy shrugged. "Apparently I can't. So now he's gone and said I could find my own way home. I think the most appropriate word to describe this situation is *stupid.*"

I made an executive decision.

"You know what, Daisy? *Screw* Bret. Okay? He sucks. You're going to hang out with us now and we're going to make this the best outing you've ever had. Ever. No questions."

Daisy looked me in the eyes and smiled weakly. I *wanted* to be there for her. I *wanted* to see her smile. It was all I wanted at this very moment.

"Then let's get out of here."

Chapter 13

We left the pizza parlor and it was almost six in the evening now. We got into Becky and had no idea where to go and what to do.

"What are we trying to do tonight?" Isaac asked.

"We could go ... laser tagging," Kimberly offered.

"But we already went bowling," pointed out Daisy.

"Who says we can't do both?"

"Do *you* want to pay for it?" Fabian said.

"Actually you're right I'm not tryna pay for anything."

"Let's go to the mall," Daisy said.

I turned Becky on and said. "Okay let's go there."

I took the AUX cord and plugged it into my phone and started to play an alternative song.

"Oh my gosh, Michael!" Isaac cried.

"Michael, no!" Fabian said. "Not this band."

"Yeah they suck."

"You have a terrible taste in music, Michael."

"Alright, you know what? *Shut up.*" I said. "You always have to say something about my taste in music."

"That's cause it *sucks,*" said Isaac.

I turned off the song and put on an indie song Isaac showed me one time.

"You like this? This is the kind of stuff you'd listen to."

"Yes. Uno is amazing."

"Yo, Uno sucks," Fabian said.

"You know what, Fabian? Shut up."

"Why do you always got to be so mean to me?"

"Why don't you *do* something about it then?"

"Well what do you want me to do … like … cry like a pansy? This has been going on since freshman year."

The girls started laughing and I was too.

"I can't stand this," I said about ten seconds later. At the next red light, I put on another rock song.

"No!" Isaac crooned.

"Shut up, Isaac. Listen to some *good* music in your life for once."

We ended up getting to the mall fifteen minutes later and I parked Becky.

"I need to get a new romper," Kimberly announced, walking into Francesca's.

"I don't understand rompers," Isaac said.

"What's there to understand?"

"Like it's just one piece of clothing which is essentially a top and shorts. Why not just wear a top and shorts?"

"'Cause … no? That requires *two* pieces of clothing. Rompers and dresses are just one piece and they flow so nicely."

"Oo look at that dress!" Daisy pointed out.

It was a black and white stripped one.

"Is that black with white stripes or white with black stripes?" Isaac *had* to ask.

"It's black with white stripes because the top one is black," Kimberly pointed out.

"That's a good answer."

"I feel like I can't pull off a dress like that," Daisy said.

"What?" Kimberly asked, appalled. "Girl, yes you can."

"I'd look like a sack of potatoes if I'd wear that."

Kimberly and Daisy started looking around and we were hovering around them.

"Look at that shirt," Isaac pointed out. I saw it was a puke green color and it was torn. "So I could cut it up right now and say that it's just part of the design."

"Hey, Maria has this dress," Fabian said.

"How *is* Maria, by the way?" I asked. It had been a while since we talked about his girlfriend.

"She's fine."

"You never talk about her, man."

"You know why. My parents got so mad at me."

"Wait, what happened?" Daisy asked.

"I went to elementary school with her and we started talking more this past year and now we're dating," Fabian explained. "And then my sister caught us together one day at the park and she told my parents and they got *so* mad at me and said I couldn't see her again."

"But you do."

Fabian nodded, looking scared.

"Don't tell anyone."

Daisy gave him a look like *what?*

"Fabian, *who* am I going to tell?"

Kimberly didn't get a romper and we left the store to go to another one called Lost Island.

"This store is awesome," I said, walking into the store and a heavy metal song was playing.

"Remember coming here when we were thirteen?" Daisy asked, coming up next to me.

I thought back to those memories. "Scene kid for life, Daisy."

"I *haate you!*" Daisy and I started laughing. It was amazing how you could think back to those times that mean everything to do. *So many inside jokes ...*

I got a band shirt that I had been wanting and Daisy bought a different band tank top. Fabian, too, bought a shirt of a cartoon show he liked.

When we left Lost Island, we were standing in a circle with our bags.

"Yo, we all look like fools right now with all these Lost Island bags," I said. "Fabian put my bag in yours so we don't look so lame."

Fabian groaned and opened his bag so I could put mine in.

"I need to get acne medicine," Kimberly said.

"You don't *have* any acne," Fabian said.

"I know but I feel like I'm going to break out 'cause my period's coming."

"You don't need acne medicine," Isaac said. "Just drink water and think yourself out of it."

"I wish it was that easy."

We walked around the mall a little bit more and we passed by a high end place for suits and tuxedos. Posters on the store's display were of guys in tuxes advertising prom.

"Who's going to prom, guys?" Daisy asked.

"I am!" Kimberly said. "It's going to be so much fun."

"I might," I said.

"I'm *not*," Fabian muttered.

"What?" Daisy asked. "Come *on!* You *have* to go!"

"No I want to go with Maria but neither of us can go with each other."

"Bro, yes you can," I told him. "We can sneak you out and everything."

Fabian shook his head. "No it's not going to work."

"We can get him fitted and everything," Kimberly told me. "And then we can pick it up, Maria can get her dress. Then just say that he's hanging out with us."

"Dude, what? My parents'll know about all that money I'll spend on a ticket and a tux. Plus Maria will have to pay more."

"I have a teal dress she could look at if she wants to wear it," Kimberly offered. "What size dress is she?'

"I don't know that. No, guys, stop. It's not gonna work."

"Oh it'll work. Plus join student council. They're doing a thing where a guy can walk around and advertise tuxedos and you can get your tux for free if you give five guys a discount card and use your name. It'll all work out perfectly."

Huh, I thought. *This might actually work.*

We ended up leaving the mall and surprisingly, it was dark outside.

"Hey, have you all ever been to Wingman's?" I asked.

"What's that?" Isaac asked.

"You've never heard of Wingman's? Okay, we're going there now."

We piled into Becky and I turned the key and the engine started to sputter.

"Oh no," I breathed. "Come on, Becky. Don't die on me."

"Let's go, *Becky!*" Isaac cried. "We're not trying to call a tow truck."

I turned the key again and it wasn't working. And I had enough gas.

"Michael, you gotta turn it with conviction and vigor," Daisy advised.

I closed my eyes, mouthed a prayer, and turned the key again. And the engine came to life.

"AYE!" everyone cheered.

I started to drive.

"Can we put the window's down?" Daisy asked.

"Yeah and let's turn the AC on," said Isaac.

Kimberly, in the passenger seat, took the AUX cord and started to play some rap music.

"This song is garbage," I said, irritated.

"Michael always hated rap music," Daisy said.

"Really?" Kimberly asked. "Why?"

"I just don't like it."

"Anybody have any pets?" Fabian asked.

"I have a hedgehog!" Daisy said.

"Oh my gosh, do you really?"

"I do!"

"What's his name?"

"His name is Hercules but I call him Kuss Kuss!"

"Aww."

"I know, he's so cute; I love him *so much.* "

In about five minutes, we reached Wingman's and I parked.

"There is so much parking lot here," Fabian observed.

"This is one of the biggest grocery stores in the area," I informed.

"I've never heard of this place," Daisy said.

"This is the first one so far but they're making more."

"Why are we at a grocery store?" Isaac asked. "Are we going grocery shopping?"

"It's all part of the experience, Isaac. You can make your own peanut butter here!"

"How do you make your own peanut butter?" Kimberly asked.

"Just come on, I'll show you."

I led everyone into Wingman's and it was just as amazing as it always was. It was a giant grocery store that seemed endless.

"Yo, look at this," I said, walking over to the frozen food section. I picked up an orange juice smoothie and showed it to everyone. "I got these every day during volleyball season. They make these from fresh oranges every morning and you know what they do with the ones they don't sell? They throw it away 'cause it's not fresh anymore."

"That's terrible," Daisy said, appalled. "Why throw away a perfectly good smoothie?"

"You buy this one and drink it and tell me how pulpy and disgusting it tastes."

I continued walking through the bakery. "You want some doughnuts?"

"Do they throw away the doughnuts at the end of the day 'cause they suck?" Daisy challenged.

"I don't know. Maybe."

I rounded a corner and walked past a salad bar that had pretty much everything in it. Olives, tomatoes, cucumbers.

"There's a five star restaurant in this place, you guys. It's upstairs."

We continued walking down the grocery store and I turned into the peanut aisle. At some point, Kimberly got into a shopping cart and Isaac was pushing her along.

"Guys, look at this. You can take whatever peanuts you want and you put it in these blender things and you can make your own peanut butter!" I picked up a container of some of it. "Look, this is *homemade* peanut butter."

"You really love this place, don't you?" Kimberly said, distractedly.

"'Cause it's awesome."

I led them down the aisle and then walked past all the registers.

"Yo, they got *ice* here?!" Isaac said with enthusiasm. "This place *does* have everything!"

I walked out of Wingman's and went back to Becky. She started and we were out of the parking lot.

"What the heck was that for, Michael?" Isaac asked, getting into the car.

"You all needed to experience Wingman's."

"Can we go to Gazzy's?" Fabian asked.

"The gas station?" Kimberly asked. "For what?"

"I'm thirsty."

"Why didn't you get anything from that Wingman's place?"

"'Cause I wasn't about to spend five dollars on a drink there!"

"No, Fabian we can't go to Gazzy's," I said and then realized I was thirsty. "Actually no let's go there. I'm thirsty."

"Gazzy's is awesome. There's this guy named Clifford that works there and he's so great," Isaac said. "He asks you about your day and everything; he's so nice."

"Bro, I would get a Gazzy's tattoo if I could," I mentioned.

"You're supposed to get tattoos of things that mean a lot to you," Daisy pointed out.

"Exactly."

"Guys, if time is money, are ATM's time machines?" Isaac wondered.

I saw Daisy cover her face with her hands. "Yes, Isaac," Daisy said. "They're time machines."

I pulled into the parking lot of Gazzy's and we went inside. I went straight to the fountain drinks and pulled out a medium sized cup and started filling it with some juice.

"Wait I want something to drink also," Isaac said, staring contemplatively at the different sized cups.

"Then get something," Kimberly said, taking a medium sized cup and walked to the fountain where I was. *"Aye, buddy, get outta da way."*

"Aye, I'm standing here. Wait your turn."

"Bro," Fabian said. "Why are there different groups of blood?"

"So mosquitos can enjoy different flavors," Isaac replied, filling his cup. Needless to say, we were hollering with laughter.

We all ended up getting drinks and after we paid, we stood around Becky and were drinking them. Kimberly was sitting cross legged on the trunk and Daisy was dangling her legs off the side of the trunk.

"You know Brian created a Socialist club?" Fabian asked.

"He is *obsessed* with communism," Kimberly said disgusted.

"I mean in theory communism isn't terrible," Isaac said. "It's just never been practiced well."

"Isn't communism where they distribute money?" Daisy asked.

"No that's socialism."

"Socialism is where they distribute money and such and communism is where they promote the general welfare," informed Fabian.

"Well anyway, Brian is weird," Daisy said. "He's got the communism flag in his room and he has the tattoo?"

"You've been in his room?" I wondered.

"No. He plays lacrosse and Bret was telling me about it."

"Anybody want to do anything else?" I offered. It wasn't that late anyway but I was pretty sure the others wanted to get home.

"Let's go to Horner Park!" Kimberly announced. "Play on the swings."

"Let's *dooo* it," Isaac said.

And then we all got back into Becky and started driving. We were off again.

"Michael, I love your car," Daisy said. "Becky's always there for us."

"I know, right?" I said. "She's awesome."

We got to Horner Park and then we all burst out of the car. We ran to the playground and it was empty for us.

I ran to the swings and sat on it and started to swing.

"Somebody push me!" Daisy said. Isaac was the closest to her and he started to push her.

"Oh my gosh, Isaac that's too high!"

Isaac stopped pushing her and ran to a soccer ball Fabian found. He kicked it to Isaac but he blocked it with his hands.

"I should join the soccer team," he said.

"Who's the greatest goalie of all time?"

Isaac snickered. "The Berlin Wall."

Fabian hollered with laughter. "Okay bet, France and Germany in the finals this year. Count on it."

"Yeah I agree and France will probably surrender."

Fabian and I started laughing.

"Was that a joke?" Daisy asked.

"Yeah," Isaac said.

"Oh. That joke was too smart for me."

I jumped off the swings and ran to join Kimberly on the slide.

"I'm having such a good time," she whispered to me.

Then we wiggled her way in between my legs and we slid down together.

And then the five of us all sprinted up the hill and we all looked up. We were breathing heavy because of all that running but it was okay since we were all together. We are the kids our parents warned us about. All friends who met in the strangest of circumstances. If this was what life was all about, I never wanted it to end.

Chapter 14

The night ended after that. I dropped everyone off home and it was just about after midnight when our night adventure ended.

I got back home, took a shower, and laid down on my bed and just laid down and was overwhelmed with just how much fun we had. Friends being together and enjoying our lives. We were young. We were free. And we had the whole world in front of us.

The next Monday morning when I came back from school, I checked the mail and saw my name on an envelope that had Milton University's logo on the top. And a sticker on it that read: *Open now! Your acceptance letter is enclosed!*

"Oh my GOSH," I breathed.

I tore open the envelope and pulled out a cardstock certificate that said *Congratulations on your acceptance to Milton University, Michael Wilson!* I took out the letter itself and it said they were going to award me a scholarship of nineteen thousand dollars.

I felt frozen. I had done it. I was in college.

Chapter 15

One Week Later

I was up late at night typing a paper for my psychology class when I honestly didn't need to but my teacher said we'd get extra credit if we wrote it. So that meant I was writing it.

Suddenly a knock came at my door.

Why are people knocking at my door at one at night?

I looked through the peephole and saw ...

I opened the door in a heartbeat and closed it behind me.

She threw herself in my arms and I held her, stroking her back. Something obviously happened.

"Michael!" she cried. "Oh my gosh, Michael ..."

"Shh," I shushed. "It's okay ..."

"No it's not!"

She pushed herself away from me and I saw tears in her eyes.

"My dad! He killed Kuss Kuss!"

"Wait, *what* happened?"

"My dad found out about Bret and I because he saw Bret drop me off this afternoon and he got so angry at me! He took Kuss Kuss' cage and he kept on shaking it in front of me and every time I tried to stop him, he pushed me away."

"Oh man … Daisy …" I wasn't sure what to say. I wasn't sure if I even *should* have said anything. "I'm so sorry. Does he know you're here?"

"No. He went out. He's not here." After several beats, she said, "Can we drive?"

I ran back inside, got my keys, and ran outside and opened up Becky. We got in and I started driving. Daisy rolled her window down and rested her chin on her arm on the ledge. We didn't say anything and I was sure she was feeling angry, broken, and trapped.

I drove up to Brisbane Cliff and turned off Becky. Daisy still rested her head on her arm and I heard her sigh.

"Daisy?" I said. "You want to talk?"

She sighed again. "No … *Yeah* … I just don't know what to talk about."

I stayed quiet and waited for her to say something. All I wanted right then and there was to hold her in my arms and do all I could to make her smile.

"Can we sit out on the hood?"

I opened the door and got a blanket from my trunk and spread it on the hood of the car. We climbed on the hood and laid down next to each other.

"If you could wish for one thing, what would it be?"

"Uh," I said dumbly. "Like material based?"

"No, anything."

"I really don't know."

"I'd wish things would go back to the way they were."

I closed my eyes and felt so much. "Daisy, this is going to sound really cheesy but you're going to experience so many good things. You're going to meet amazing people and fall in love so many times and do so many things. A phase of something negative isn't the end to the endless possibilities awaiting you."

"It's funny you say how I'm going to fall in love so many times."

Maybe that was a wrong choice of words.

"I know things were bad with you and Alex. And I know what happened with Spencer."

"A cheater and a guy who lost interest in me."

"He didn't lose interest in *you*. Spencer just sucks."

I heard her sigh with laughter. "You know even though I've been burned out by bad relationships in the past, I think Bret and I are meant to be. I know that sounds cheesy but it's true."

I closed my eyes. "Are you really, Daisy?"

"I don't know. I don't *feel* anything genuine with him."

"Then what keeps you with him?"

"Probably because he's the only guy that cared for me."

I care for you.

"Daisy, just 'cause some guy gives you attention in that way doesn't mean you have to give him everything."

"I know it doesn't."

"So?"

"So what? I can't seem to get out of this."

"I think you can. Just tell him you're not interested in being with him anymore."

"Then that'll make me sound me like Spencer."

"No it won't, Daisy. It'll save you instead of torturing yourself another day by being with that *Bret.*"

She sighed again. "How are you doing? You know, with Malachi and that situation?"

Only Daisy could get to the heart of the matter like that.

"It's okay. I mean him not being here is always going to hurt but it's not like I can change what's happened. Imagine it like a story. The death is like a supporting character in the background that doesn't *directly* affect the life of the main character but it affects him in everything else he does."

"That's an interesting way to look at it. You know something crazy? My dad blames *me* for my mom dying. *Me!* Just because she got cancer after I was born it's suddenly *my* fault."

"Daisy, you know it's not your fault."

"And he says I'm a failure because my grades aren't what he wants them to be."

"You're *number twenty eight* in the class."

"Not good enough for him."

"You *are* good enough, Daisy."

"It feels like no one wants me around anymore." She stayed silent after I said that. It was so hard to believe the girl I once knew who was so in love with life was now struggling to find sense in all of it.

"Even though things suck for me, I'm so happy. Like that night we had last week? It was so much fun! I had such a good time. You, Isaac and Fabian are so stupid."

I closed my eyes and replayed the memories and smiled. I was happy for her to be happy.

She suddenly sat up right and I heard the sound of pills in a capsule. I sat up too and saw her holding the bottle, rubbing her thumb over the label. The capsule was full.

"Can I tell you a story?" her tone was quieter now.

"Sure."

"Earlier in the year for gym, we had our swimming unit and I have Sydney in that class."

"Sydney?"

"She's a Lax Girl."

The girl who was celebrating the Lax Bros' one victory. "So *that's* her name."

"Well anyway, she's been mean to me. She'd say rude things to me and bad mouthing me. And one day, my mom took me to the thrift store 'cause that's the only place where we can afford to buy clothes and I got name brand jeans and a sweater. They were my new clothes. I wore them to school one day and when I came back from showering from swimming, I couldn't find them. I was running around trying to find them, panicking that I'd be late to class and everything. I saw Sydney walk out of the bathroom and she looked directly at me. Then I saw my clothes in the toilet.

"Ms. McQueen told me *I* had to fish them out and put them in this plastic bag. Then I had to wear my gym uniform for the rest of the day. Well I didn't have it so I had to borrow an extra extra large shirt from them. Do you understand how *humiliating* that was, Michael? Walking around school in those extra huge clothes and gym ones at that? Everyone was staring at me."

"I'm so sorry to hear that, Daisy," I said with a broken heart.

"As things went, I got him and threw away the bag because they were practically worthless and dirty at that point. I felt so ... *I felt so* ... I felt ..."

And then I scooted over and put my arm around her. She was stiff at first and then softened and leaned into my shoulder.

"I felt broken."

"Daisy, you deserve so much better."

She looked at the pills again. "I've never been so hurt in my whole life. Maybe I should have seen this coming but I never felt so hopeless than I do tonight. I'm living everyday drowning in my mind. I don't want to live like this anymore; I'm moving on."

"Good. I'm proud of you."

"I mean … at some point, everyone's heartstrings come undone."

I nodded. "At least once."

"But even when my heartstrings come undone, I will stay with you." She stuck out her pinky. I wrapped my pinky around hers.

Daisy took her pinky back. She pulled her arm back, and flung it forward, throwing the pills off Brisbane Cliff. The capsule went sailing and it was out of sight in seconds. Silence filled the space between us. She was breathing slowly but heavily.

She turned to look me in the eyes and said, "It's all a matter of perspective. It's like what Isaac said about acne medicine. If I thought my way into this, I can think my way out of it."

"Just drink water and think your way out of it," I repeated with a smile.

"Exactly. I don't need those pills." She pointed at the edge of the cliff. "I can cure this by myself. I can cure it with good times and good vibes."

"With good friends," I added.

"And of course, *good friends.*"

We smiled and I looked at her lips. Maybe somewhere deep down inside of me, I knew we'd never end up as something more than friends. But even at that, we weren't friends for a long time. Yet here we were. What did that make us now? What would it make us in the future?

"I feel so *great!*" Daisy cheered. "Michael, let's do something crazy."

"You mean go home and go to sleep?" I suggested, mostly because I was getting a little tired.

"Sleep? What is that? Michael, we are sleepwalkers."

I was always up for a night time adventure.

"What should we do?" I asked.

"Anything and everything. Tonight is *our* night. Just you and me. Let's take over the world."

We smiled at each other and then we ran off in the night.

Chapter 16

At this point, I have started to like Becky more because she was always there for me and always ready to go at any given moment. I said that she was a lemon and pretty stupid as a car. But now I was happy to have Becky. Without her, I wouldn't be able to get to and fro easily, nor would I be able to have night adventures with my friends.

Daisy and I had the best night of our life. They were just like old times. But instead of sitting on the couch and watching movies and eating pizza, now that we were older, we went out driving. I took her to this place called Lake Geneva and we went swimming.

We stripped to our underwear jumped into the lake while holding hands. At that point, we were best friends, attached at the hip, inseparable, thick as thieves just like old times.

We ran out of the lake and we hugged and spun around. She locked her fingers with mine and pushed. I stumbled backwards, and then pushed her back. Daisy threw her head back and let out a howl of laughter. We were there pushing against each other until we both fell down and were hollering with laughter.

"We're pretty terrible," Daisy said, laughing.

A little while later, we washed the sand on our bodies in the water. And then stood there for a minute, looking at each other. A shadow fell across Daisy's face and she walked towards me and pulled me into a hug.

We stood there for I don't know how long just holding each other in the lake, the sounds of the water gently lapping the shore, the moonlight shining down on us. I gently scratched her back and she tensed for a second and then relaxed against me. She started running her fingers in my hair at the nape of my skull.

"Sorry," she said, after we dis-embraced. "I just really needed that."

"It's okay."

We got back to Becky and sat inside. I turned the heat on full blast as we waited for our clothes and our bodies to dry.

Then I saw a flashlight.

"Cops?" Daisy asked, pointing outside my window.

I looked and saw two flashlight beams heading towards us. We were about to get busted.

"Okay, hang on," I said. I turned the key and Becky roared to life. I reversed quickly and jerked the wheel to the left. I saw the flashlight beams go haywire, trying to stop us.

"Go, go, go, go!" Daisy was shouting.

"Hey! Hey, stop!"

I put the car in drive and floored it. We raced past the police and I continued driving fast. Daisy, the ever thoughtful one, plugged her phone into the AUX cord and she blasted music as we drove off in the night. Never underestimate the therapeutic power of driving through the night listening to music.

We were partners in crime and I was mad for her. We were the kids our parents warned us about.

"Okay, I'm getting kinda hot now," Daisy said, turning the heat off and putting on her tank top. "I think we lost them."

"Good."

"Pull over, put some clothes on."

I pulled over and tugged my shirt over my head and put my shorts on. Daisy wriggled into her shorts.

"Maybe one day … we can actually try skinny dipping."

"Let's *not.* I'm not trying to get infected or anything."

After Lake Geneva, I drove to Gazzy's and Clifford was there.

"Isn't it kinda late?" Clifford asked.

"Kinda," I replied.

"And isn't it a school night?"

"Yeah?"

Clifford shrugged. "I suppose."

Daisy and I got pop and candy and we paid for them. Then we sat in Becky and started eating and drinking. We were getting sugar drunk.

"Remember that time our families had Easter dinner together?" she asked.

I laughed. "That's the day I got a nosebleed!"

"Hahahaha. You texted me you were like 'my nose is bleeding. Help.'"

We laughed and laughed over and over and over; we were high on life. This was living. In this life, you only meet a couple people who speak to your soul and set you free. All we have is what's in between hello and goodbye. To write someone's, happiness, we must do our best to erase their past. And that's what Daisy and I were for each other.

"This is actually very therapeutic," she said. "Screw those pills."

"Let's just spend every day like this," I said, speaking my mind. "You and me and nothing but the road ahead. Day dreaming and night thinking."

She stayed quiet after I said that and I was starting to think I shouldn't have. She was with Bret. I was nothing but her friend. And that was okay because being friends with someone is sometimes all the connection you need with a person.

"Alright!" I said, diffusing the awkwardness. "Where do we want to go next?" I checked the time and it was only three forty one in the morning. We certainly were sleepwalkers.

"I doubt we can go to school tomorrow," Daisy said.

"Not that it really matters anymore."

"What are you doing after you graduate?"

"I'm going to Milton."

"Oh so you got in?"

"Yeah. I was so happy to find out."

And then the very real thought of us going away to college came into my mind. How we were going to separate after nearly nine years of friendship.

"Let's go to Horner Park," I announced.

"Okay."

I turned on Becky to get to the park. I parked and we got out. Daisy ran, jumped the fence, and ran straight for the swings. I was right on her heels.

"Push me!" she ordered.

"But I wanted to swing too," I complained.

"Ugh, fine."

So we swung together, trying to get higher than the other.

"You suck, Daisy," I said as I was at the level of the branches.

"Shut up," she said as we passed each other on the way down.

I slowed down my swinging speed and jumped off and ran up the slide. I saw Daisy still swinging. I slid down the slide and then Daisy jumped off her swing. She stumbled and ran to stop herself.

"I'm getting really tired now," she said.

"Really? I'm so super hyper and awake right now."

"Let's go back to Becky."

We got back to Becky and opened the doors. We sat down and just sat there for a while. It was now four sixteen and we were clearly exhausted.

I still couldn't believe we were doing this.

"Did you hear about the gorilla that got shot?" Daisy asked.

"Yeah. I still think it's the mom's fault for not watching her kid."

"I know, right! Stupid mom. She shouldn't even *be* a mom. Plus wasn't the gorilla like some endangered species or something?"

"I don't know for sure."

"Either way I think it's depressing."

"Well yeah but tell me why that story got so much media coverage and the story about the man who shot a guy who was trying to shoot up a night club didn't get any media attention?"

"Wait what happened?"

"See what I mean? In Tennessee, this guy walked in and shot four people but this one guy stopped him and it got zero media coverage. Just because it wasn't like fifty people dying or something. Plus their doing research and stuff on how to better protect animals. I love animals, don't get me wrong, but they're doing so much for a gorilla, what about *people?*"

"Did you hear about that police officer who shot the guy at point blank range."

I scoffed. "Which *one*. It seems like every week there's some cop killing an innocent person."

"It's racism all over again. It's basically the 1960s happening in today's times."

"It is. Plus it's murder."

"It's so terrible that the people we look up to for protection and security let us down."

I leaned my head against the headrest. "I disagree about it being self-defense. None of the people who've been killed have posed any sort of threat to the cops whatsoever. And you're going to say you *thought* they were reaching for your gun?! You just *shot* someone!"

"This world sucks," she summed up.

"Pretty much."

"Plus about the whole murder thing … it's not right to kill anyone."

"Murder is unlawful killing so like in wars, it's okay."

"War is *not* okay!"

"I didn't mean okay like acceptable but when it comes to it, when in war, you're killing for your country."

"War doesn't justify killing someone."

"I know it doesn't but when in a time of war, then you're doing it for self-defense and the safety of your nation."

"Are you being serious right now? War isn't something that *should* happen in the first place. All those veterans that come back suffering from PTSD 'cause of all the horrors of war? That's not okay at all!"

"Look if it were up to me, war wouldn't exist but it's here so we have to deal with it."

Daisy exhaled sharply and looked away. Nighttime *is* when the best conversations happen, though.

"So what do you think about the death penalty?" I asked.

"The death penalty? I think it's messed up! Just kill someone just because they did something wrong? No that's so messed up. And ... sending a kid to jail for five years because they found half a pound of marijuana on him doesn't make sense to me either."

"I agree I think there needs to be a reform in the whole Justice System."

"Okay you know what I *don't* understand?" Daisy asked, whirling around. "Sports."

"What?" I asked, not believing her.

"No like not how to *play* sports. All the money that goes into it. These players are getting tens of millions of dollars to play sports which is great but what if for one year, we stopped all those sports and put all that money to doing other things."

"Other things like?"

"Like infrastructure or funding new forms of cleaner energy, things that could benefit the nation."

104

"That sounds like a good idea in theory but it can't be practiced 'cause nobody's going to give up that money to put it towards the things you just said."

"Yeah that's actually right."

"What's your biggest fear?" Radom, I know.

Daisy paused. "My biggest fear? I guess it would be … abandonment."

"Why so?"

"I chose that word because it means to leave completely. It means you once had somebody. And then when they leave you … you're totally alone. And all you have are those memories and feelings of what it felt like to be with them. Then they abandon you and you're all by yourself. I guess that's what I fear most. What's *your* biggest fear?"

"My biggest fear isn't really a fear, as such."

"What is it?"

"I'm afraid of attaching myself to other people in the hopes that they will like and appreciate me for who I am."

"I'm afraid my problems and concerns are trivial and not worth the time of other people."

"I'm afraid that my friends are closer with each other than they are with me. Isaac and Fabian … they've known each other since freshman year and I just met them in September."

"I'm afraid that I spend so much time doing things now to feel proud about in the future that I don't feel happy now, in the moment. Like when I sit down, I don't really know who I am because I'm always working, always studying, always trying to be something. I'm afraid of only focusing on who I want to be that I don't know who I am. I've spent so much time trying to get into Rockford and focusing on that."

I didn't say anything more even though I have many fears. Everything we want is on the other side of fear.

"You know what's funny?" Daisy asked. "Life."

"What about it?"

"Life is ironic. It takes sadness to know happiness. Noise to appreciate silence. And absence to appreciate presence. And Michael? About not being close with your friends? Not everyone is going to make it into your future. Some people are just passing along to teach you lessons about life."

Daisy truly was wise and hearing that was very encouraging. It was actually pretty depressing but I needed to hear that.

"And about your future? Sometimes the best thing you can do is not think, not wonder, not obsess. Just breathe and have faith that everything is going to work out for the best."

Five o' clock in the morning.

The sky was starting to turn bright with the first rays of sunlight. It was hard to believe that just a short while ago, we were sitting on Brisbane Cliff.

"Alright, Michael," Daisy said. "I think it's time we get home."

I was so wide awake but I was so dang exhausted so I agreed. I drove back to my house and parked Becky. We got out and then we hugged for what seemed like five minutes. At that point, time didn't exist for us.

"You're not going to school, are you?" I asked.

She shook her head, disgusted. "Oh gosh no. Not today."

"Same."

She smiled at me. "I'll see you later," she said.

Your eyes drive me crazy.

She crossed the street and walked in her house and I prayed her father wouldn't yell at her or anything. I snuck back into my house and made a beeline to my room where I shut the door and laid down on my bed, overwhelmed with how alive I felt.

I didn't fall asleep instantly. Instead I looked at my ceiling and replayed everything that happened in the past few hours. The cliff, Lake Geneva, getting our sugar rush, the park, the conversations … it was all amazing. It was transcendent. It was marvelous.

I knew I wouldn't be going to school tomorrow I closed my eyes and fell asleep peacefully for the first time in a very long time.

Chapter 17

I didn't wake up till three in the afternoon and that was because my phone was ringing.

"Ah?" I said as a greeting.

"Michael Wilson," Isaac said firmly. "Where the heck were you today, you *walrus?"*

"What … what *time* is it?"

"It's half past we're all mad at you. You missed the planning for Fabian's prom night."

I dropped my head on the pillow and said, "Okay, come by my house in an hour."

"Alright, we'll be there."

I hung up and laid on my bed and let out a long sigh. I got out of bed and opened my door. I saw a handwritten note taped to it: *you were asleep like a rock this morning and you missed school. We'll talk when I get back from work …*

Oh great.

Maybe my mom knew about me sneaking out late at night. I'd be dead if she found out. Not to mention take Becky away from me.

Not Becky.

I tried not to think about it as I took a shower and got ready. I knew I missed a lot of material in school but it was okay. We were basically three weeks away from graduation and I was already set to go to Milton University in August.

At four o' clock on the dot, the others were at my door. Isaac, Fabian, and Kimberly.

"I've never been in your house, Michael," Kimberly said, surveying my living room. "It's pretty."

"Thanks."

"What I really mean is what's the Wi-Fi password."

I gave it to her.

"Alright," Isaac said, sitting down on my couch. "Why weren't you in school?"

I told them everything.

"So *did* you go skinny dipping?" Isaac questioned. "'Cause that's dangerous, man. You don't know what's in that water."

"So we didn't go skinny dipping," I confirmed. She's not going to tell Bret or anything. And this just stays between us."

"For sure," Fabian said.

"But that sounds like so much fun," Kimberly said. "I wish *I* could've come."

"It was really a lot of fun."

"Well that's good but we've got a prom plan to discuss."

They told me the plan. How Fabian would pay for the ticket and how'd he get his tux. Maria would have to find a way to sneak out too and it worked perfectly. It just might have worked out.

And what's the plan? Oh yeah like I'll tell *you?*

That evening when my mom came back from work, she wasted no time.

"You didn't go to school today," she said. She was asking me and telling me at the same time.

"No," I told her. "I guess I was too exhausted."

I held my breath, hoping she wouldn't figure out how I snuck out of the house late last night to be with Daisy.

She sighed. "I know you've been working so hard this past year, Michael. With volleyball *and* school? It's been tough on you. I understand. Don't worry. It's okay."

Well then.

Chapter 18

I *can* tell you one part of the plan.

On that weekend, we had to go to the tuxedo place to get Fabian fitted.

"I don't know about this, you guys ..." Fabian kept on saying.

"Shut up," Kimberly told him. "You're going to be having the time of your life at prom. And ... your friends are doing the most for you right now so *you're welcome.*"

We explained to the guy who we were and how Fabian was going to be modeling tuxedos for our school and the people at the shop quickly got him fitted.

"Are you two modeling tuxedos also?" the guy asked Isaac and I. But since we weren't in student council, we had to say we weren't.

Then my phone started ringing.

I went out of the store and answered it.

"Michael?" Daisy's scared voice was on the other end.

"Hey, what's up? Where are you? We're all the mall getting Fabian –"

"Can you come to the hospital?"

"What happened?"

There was silence in the background for a few seconds and then Daisy said, "Just come" and then she hung up.

I went back into the store and I don't know what my expression looked like but Kimberly said, "What happened?"

"Daisy just called, she's at the hospital."

"What? What happened?"

"I don't know but I'm going to see what happened."

Kimberly pursed her lips. "Okay. I can finish things here. Let us know what happens."

"I'll come with you," Isaac said.

Kimberly put a hand on my shoulder. "Be careful."

We walked/jogged to Becky and got inside. Fear and panic coursed through my veins; my heart started to beat rapidly.

"You okay?" Isaac asked.

I swallowed a lump in my throat and nodded. Then I began to drive, hoping Daisy was okay.

Chapter 19

"It's nothing, Michael, just a broken wrist. I'll be fine."

She was holding onto her left wrist which had a cast on it. A woman who I assumed was her step mother was in the waiting room with her. I also saw Bret sitting in a chair, sitting cross legged, looking … content.

"What happened?" I asked.

"Nothing. We were driving and then he lost control of the wheel … then I broke my wrist."

They got into a car accident. My heart was still beating quickly and it felt like it would explode.

"I'm fine, don't worry."

"Okay," Bret said suddenly. He stood up and walked to where we were standing. "I'm not doing this anymore."

"What?" Daisy asked.

"This," he repeated. "You and I. This. I'm sick of it."

"Bret … what are you talking about?"

"Isn't it obvious?"

"You're saying you wanna break up?"

"Thought it was kinda obvious."

Daisy's eyes widened and I could tell tears were coming on.

Don't cry, I tried to send telepathically to her.

"Apparently not to me."

"Well sorry you didn't catch on. I don't know what else you want me to do."

Daisy pursed her lips and they started to quiver. She wanted to say something but wasn't sure what to say. Then Bret walked out of the waiting room.

She turned to me and she … smiled.

"I'm just glad *I* didn't have to say it."

Chapter 20

The next few weeks went by quickly.

Nothing much happened except for Fabian walking around school one day to model his tux. He handed out his discount cards to other guys and we hoped five of them would use his name that way he'd get his rental for free. Needless to say, Isaac and I would be using his discount cards.

Kimberly had her teal prom dress from last year; Maria and her had a fitting party and after a few stitches, it fit Maria perfectly.

The only thing left was the tickets ...

"Alright so this is how it's going to go down," Fabian explained one day during lunch when we were all sitting together. He had been getting excited about prom these past few weeks. "I told my parents a singer is coming to town and I wanted to get tickets. And tickets are a hundred dollars."

"Oh I see where you're going with this," Isaac said. "But continue."

Fabian nodded. "Yup. So I'm going to get my prom ticket and disguise it as buying concert tickets."

"Nice," Daisy commented. "But are you paying cash?"

"That's the interesting part. I took out a hundred dollars from the ATM and am going to buy my ticket. But I told my parents I was going straight to the box office to get tickets. That way they won't get suspicious about anything."

"Fabian, you conniving little walrus," Isaac said. "That's brilliant."

He smiled, satisfied he came up with it.

"What about Maria?" I asked. "Her ticket?"

"Same thing. Some artist is coming to town and she's going to buy tickets."

"Ohhh," Daisy said. "Are you sure this mysterious Maria exists?"

"Yes, she exists."

"Picture?"

"I don't have any pictures of her ..."

Daisy smirked. "Hmm. I don't know ..."

"Just you wait," Kimberly added. "I'm going to do her makeup too and this girl is gonna *slay.*"

Daisy was totally fine after the break up. She didn't show any signs of missing Bret or anything. Either she was taking this really well or she was secretly broken on the inside. Knowing Daisy, it was a combination of both.

When the bell rang, both Kimberly and Daisy left the lunchroom to their lockers and straight home. That left Isaac, Fabian, and myself together. It seemed like forever when it was just the three of us.

"Guys, I didn't want to bring this up in front of the others," Isaac started. "But prom dates."

"Yes," I said.

"I don't have anyone to take."

116

"You don't *need* someone to go with, Isaac."

"I know I *don't* but I think it'll be fun if I did."

"Well who were you thinking of?"

"Um … well first things first, Michael, you've got to ask Kimberly."

I rolled my eyes. "This isn't about me right now, Isaac."

"Okay fine … I was thinking about asking Sydney."

"Lax Girl Sydney?"

"Yeah."

"Dude, no. Not her."

I remembered what Daisy told me about how she tried to flush her clothes down the toilet.

"But … she's awesome. She's good at lacrosse and she's pretty …"

"And she sucks," I interrupted. "You wanna know what she did? Daisy wore new clothes one day and then Sydney put them in the toilet. They were all soaking wet and nasty."

"Yo, Sydney sucks," Fabian added. "I had her in a group project sophomore year and she didn't do any of the work."

"Okay clearly nobody likes Sydney here so I won't ask her."

"Hey, Isaac? Remember that time you got kicked out of Triangle 2?"

Isaac started laughing. "You can't kick me out and then add Jackson and Paul."

"Wait …" I said. "Triangle 2? Isn't that the club they shut down?"

"Yeah it was an all girl's service program," Isaac explained. "But they have 5 guy sweethearts they pick. And I was picked but I never did anything."

Fabian laughed. "He never did anything but always showed up to the meetings."

"Ava, who's the leader, was like 'hey Isaac, you're out of the club 'cause you never do anything.' And *then* she allowed Jackson and Paul to be part of Triangle 2."

"Jackson?" I asked. "Ava's boyfriend?"

"Yeah," Isaac said. "So she let him be part of the group and Paul is Jackson's bro or whatever."

"And then you still showed up to all the meetings," Fabian added.

"Yeah! I did! They also had these point sheets and I secretly gave myself points. Even though they kicked me out. And then eventually, Mr. Collins shut down the club because … I guess the club stopped doing service projects. But *anyway* ... back to the topic of prom dates … Michael, you have to ask Kimberly."

"Dude, no," I said.

"She likes you. You haven't seen it but the way she looks at you? The way she talks to you? You both are perfect."

"Oh my gosh."

118

"At least thing about it."

"Fuggitabouit," I said in my New York accent.

"See!" Fabian cried. "You don't do anything like that with anyone else!"

"No dude, listen," I said seriously. "Kimberly and I are just good friends, alright? There's nothing more between us than just that."

Isaac stared at me and then at each other. Isaac shrugged. "Okay, bro, whatever you say."

Eventually we left school and I headed back home, thinking about Kimberly.

Chapter 21

Two days later, Kimberly and I were left alone at the lunch table because the others had other plans. Isaac left to go home because he wanted to sleep. Fabian was going to give Maria her prom ticket. And Daisy was who knows where. She had become strangely distant ever since the car accident.

"So what's up?" I asked casually.

She shrugged. "Nothing really ... just chillin' waiting for prom and then graduation."

"What comes after graduation?"

"I'm going to Harvey White College."

"What's your major?"

"I don't know yet. I was thinking criminal justice or something with forensics. What about you?"

"I don't know either to be honest. I haven't really thought much about it."

"Well you better get on that. This is your future we're talking about."

The thought about my future and what comes next overwhelmed me.

"You alright?"

"I always liked the idea of my future ... until it started happening."

"What do you mean?"

"Like … everything's changing too fast. I can't seem to keep up?'

"Are you talking about *school?* Or Daisy? Or what?"

"Both, I guess. First her mom dies, then my brother dies. Things cycle down for the two of us and we weren't really there for each other. Then things changed again and now again and it's like we never stopped being friends."

Kimberly nodded slowly. "I get you. But you know that things change and people change. The ones you thought will always be there for you suddenly carry on with their own lives."

"Yeah," I sighed. "It's life …"

"But it's a good life, Michael."

"Tell me something? Are you afraid of the future?"

Kimberly's eyes widened. "No? I mean … not really."

"I think I am."

Kimberly gave me one of those pity looks. "You're not afraid of the future, you're afraid of repeating the past."

I looked her in the eyes. She really was pretty. But not just on the surface. Her mind was beautiful. She loved you and made you love her.

"Look," she continued. "The best part about life is not knowing what'll happen. We're all just along for the ride. The best way to live is to take on each day as it is given to us."

She sounded a lot like Daisy. She taught me how to live. She taught me that life is beautiful. That it's a beautiful life.

"Siempre pa'lante," she said.

"What?"

"Siempre pa'lante. It means always forward. Like you have to keep moving forward. The first part's just an abbreviation but it basically means keep moving forward."

"That was pretty wise of you, Kimberly Avocado," I said with a smirk, easing the depth of the conversation.

"Did you think my head was just full of hot hair?"

We chuckled.

"Hey, why don't you give me some credit, eh?"

"Well look what came offa the street? A wise gal! Ain't seen too many of those."

Kimberly's jaw dropped and she looked away, shaking her head. "So you believe in the patriarchy."

I laughed. "No I'm just kidding *with ya.*"

It really surprised me that sometimes you meet people towards the end of school you'd wish you'd met years before.

I took a deep breath and let it go.

"Do you have a date to prom?"

Chapter 22

The big night was two days away and the final preparations were being made. Fabian got his tuxedo and it matched Maria's teal dress. Isaac was going solo he was being a good sport about it.

As for me?

Kimberly agreed to go with me and we matched our outfits. She was going to wear a black and silver dress and I got a black bow tie to match. Thanks to Fabian and his discount cards, Isaac and I were able to get out rentals for a cheaper price.

Daisy had been MIA for a while but one day, she appeared for lunch and spilled some news.

"I into Rockford!"

"Oh my gosh, Daisy, congratulations!" Kimberly squeaked.

"Aye, nice job, Daisy," Isaac congratulated.

"Thanks, you guys." Then she looked me in the eyes. "So I'll be going down there after graduation because I'm renting an apartment."

"By yourself?" Fabian asked. "How much is rent? You don't have to answer that."

Daisy giggled. "No it's okay. Rent is eight hundred a month. But my landlord and I made a deal: I can pay four hundred a month if I babysit his kids."

"Dude that's really awesome," Isaac breathed. "Things're really working out for you, aren't they?"

Thankfully Isaac said that so I didn't have to. Her saying that made it very real. She was leaving.

Daisy nodded. "They are. Plus with all the financial aid stuff and scholarships and everything, I'm basically getting a full ride."

More cheers from the group.

"Daisy, I want to be you when I grow up," Isaac praised. "How'd you *do* it?"

"Hard work and dedication to who I want to be. Live your life with conviction and vigor."

"That's really great, Daisy," Kimberly added. "I'm happy for you."

Daisy looked at me again. She wanted me to tell her how happy I was for her. And I was. It was just I'd miss her.

"This is awesome, Daisy," I said. "You deserved it."

She really knew what I meant. She deserved so much better than what she had been dealt these past few years. And now with college starting for her, she had the chance to re-invent herself.

"It's only fitting that we celebrate," Daisy said.

"We *are* going to celebrate," Kimberly said firmly. "At prom!"

Chapter 23

Today was the big day.

Fabian told his parents he was going to hang out with me and might spend the night. His parents were cool about it so he rushed over to my house where two days before, he stashed his tuxedo in my closet. Once he came over, he said, "Michael, I am freaking out right now. What if I get caught? What'll happen? I am going *to die tonight and it's all your fault!"*

"Fabian, you're not gonna get caught," I assured him. "And if you do, then it'll make for a great story."

Long story short, we both spent the day getting ready and making sure we looked our best. While we were getting ready, Maria drove herself to Kimberly's house. Again, she told her parents she was going to sleep over at a friend's house.

There was so much excitement in the air. What if Fabian *did* get caught?

Screw it, I thought. This was going to be so much fun.

Once we were all ready, I drove to Kimberly's house where we were meeting up.

And that's when I saw Maria for the first time.

Her hair was up, her makeup was stunning and she looked very pretty.

"Hey," Fabian said, taking her into his arms.

Then I saw Kimberly walk out of her house. She looked resplendent in her dress. Her makeup was perfect and she looked absolutely ethereal.

"Yes, girl, slay," Kimberly said to Maria.

Isaac showed up a little while later and the first thing he said was, "I want everyone here to know that I am an independent man who don't need no woman."

Kimberly and I did the traditional corsage and boutonniere exchange and so did Fabian and Maria. We made Isaac take pictures.

"Aww, poor Isaac!" Maria said. Isaac looked at her like, *excuse me?*

"Isaac, come here," Kimberly said, extending her hand. "Michael, take a picture of us."

Maria and Kimberly stood on either side of Isaac and put their hands on his shoulder and leaned in him. I took a few pictures and handed Kimberly her phone back.

"Please don't put all these pictures on social media," Fabian worried. "I don't need the wrong people seeing them."

"Wrong people like who?" Kimberly asked.

"Like my sister. She'll tell my parents and world war three will break out."

Kimberly looked at Maria and she nodded. "Fine," Kimberly agreed. "I'll only put up the ones of us." She began tapping away on her phone.

"Besides, social media is a waste of time," Maria added.

"What's that? Sorry I couldn't hear you. I was on social media."

That got us laughing a bit.

"Okay but like where's Daisy?" Isaac asked no one in particular.

"She was supposed to be here like twenty minutes ago," Kimberly said, checking her phone. "Someone call her."

"Michael, do it," Isaac ordered.

I pulled out my phone and called her. I went straight to voicemail.

"Nothing?" Kimberly asked.

"No." I called again. Nothing.

"Well Becky is here so we're ready to go whenever we're ready."

"We should have left ten minutes ago," Fabian said. "It'll take us forty five minutes to get there. *And* it's rush hour so it'll take us longer."

"Daisy where *are* you?" I pleaded.

"If she's not here in the next seven minutes," Kimberly said, "we're leaving."

I called her for the fourth time and she *finally* answered.

"Hello?" she said.

"Daisy? Where are you?"

"Um … What?"

"We're all here at Kimberly's house … waiting for you."

"Oh. Oh. Right. Sorry. I'm already on my way there. To the hotel."

"You're on your way to the hotel?"

That got the others' attention.

"Yeah," she said distractedly. I could hear loud music in the background. "I'll meet you all there."

Then she hung up.

I put my phone in my pocket and told them what she said.

"She's already on her way," Kimberly stated, trying to make sense of it.

"So she ditched us?" Isaac pointed out.

"It would seem so," I said.

"Well *that* was certainly rude of her. We had been planning this for *weeks!*"

I felt crushed for some reason.

"You alright, Michael?" Kimberly asked, rubbing my back.

"Yeah," I swallowed. "Yeah, let's just get there. There'll be a lot of traffic."

Chapter 24

We reached the hotel and we all got out of Becky. Isaac and I held the doors open for the ladies – and Fabian – to walk through. We showed our IDs to the ladies at the desk and they made sure we were on the list.

The theme was the 1920s and it was decorated as so. 1920s swing music was playing and all the seniors from my school were in the lobby, all dressed up, looking their best. There was a red carpet that led into the foyer and above it read: *The Great Goodbye.* Off to the side was a punch bowl with a ladle to scoop into a cup.

We walked into the ballroom where the table were set. Each table had a baby blue table cloth with white plates and silverware on it. Wine styled glasses were on the table too in addition to four vases with white flowers. There were four other tables spread around the ballroom with larger white flowers and some people were huddled around them too.

"Let's find a table," Kimberly said.

We found one near the dancefloor and the ladies put their clutch purses on the seats to claim it as ours.

"I still wonder where that traitor Daisy ran off too," Isaac muttered, mostly to me. Probably because he knew I was thinking the same thing.

We went out to the lobby where Fabian and I had the pleasure of pouring punch for everyone in our party.

"Kimberly!" the girl I recognized from the party chirped, came up to us. *"Ooo gurl okay I see you."*

The two took a picture and then she took one of Kimberly and me.

"By the way, you two look so cute together," she said before dashing away.

We looked at each other. "I guess we're cute, Michael."

"Hey, look who it is," Isaac said.

I turned my head to see Daisy walking into the lobby surrounded by some people I didn't know. She looked … well, she looked amazing. She was wearing a red strapless dress and her hair was in curls and her lips were red. She usually had bags under her eyes, but tonight, she didn't. The dress was long she was wearing black heels that made her legs look elongated. She looked slender.

"Wow she looks *purty,*" Isaac mumbled.

"Isaac, shut *up.*"

She spotted me and walked right over.

"Hey," she said.

"Hey."

"Sorry about what happened. Last minute changes, you know?"

I nodded. "Yeah I mean we've only been planning this for three weeks now."

Her lips were parted as if she was about to say something.

"Never mind," I said, looking away. "It's whatever now."

She pursed her lips and joined up with the friends she came in with.

"Don't be so mad at her, Michael," Kimberly advised.

She was right.

We went back to the ballroom when eventually dinner was served.

"Yo, this ain't broccoli," Isaac noted. He stabbed it with his fork and held it two centimeters from his plate. "This is a tree."

"They probably put chemicals in it to make it this big," Fabian said.

I looked across the dancefloor and saw Daisy with her friends. She was laughing and smiling and having a grand time.

"Michael?" Kimberly said. "What are you looking at?"

I blinked.

"Nothing."

I went back to eating but something told me Kimberly knew who I was looking at.

Chapter 25

The music started at once and everyone rushed to the dance-floor. Kimberly and I held hands and we were jumping, swaying, and dancing to the music. It was loud. It was crowded. And it was so much fun. I could feel the beat of the music in my chest and whenever Kimberly or I tried to talk, we had to practically yell in each other's ears.

How much fun it was.

And then I had to go to the bathroom.

I went and then when I came back. I couldn't find Kimberly in the crowd. So I stood off to the side, trying to scout her out. And then I did.

She was dancing.

With Bret.

Interesting, I thought. And when I say *dancing* I mean grinding.

After she was done grinding with Bret, she found her girl friend from the party and then *they* began to "dance" together. Soon after, another guy came up to Kimberly and she happily "danced" with him. Then another guy. And two other girls.

"Dancing is a sin," Isaac said, coming up behind me.

"What?" I asked. "No."

"Then why aren't you out there ... *sinning?* "

"Uh ..."

I tried to talk but then I saw Daisy and Bret dancing.

"Oh I see," Isaac said. "What about Kimberly?"

"She's off dancing with other people."

"That's okay, right? She can dance with other people."

"Yeah it's fine."

"Hm. Well I *would* invite you to dance, but I don't believe in sinning."

I laughed and followed him outside where we got punch and ice cream.

"I still think it kinda sucks Daisy broke her wrist and then her boyfriend broke up with her," he pointed out.

I shrugged. "You heard her. She said she was glad he did it and not her."

"But now they're doing their best to become one being, if you know what I mean."

I smiled sadly. "She told me she didn't really like him. But here she is, going after him again."

After a few seconds of silence, Isaac asked, "What about Kimberly?"

"What about her?"

"You asked her to prom."

"So?"

"So do you like her or are you two here just as friends?"

I honestly didn't know. It seemed we were here as friends than anything else.

"Just friends," I told him.

"So maybe she *doesn't* like you. But you feel what towards her?"

"Nothing. Well not *nothing* but nothing like that."

"Gotcha. Sorry for insisting that she liked you."

"It's okay."

"But tell me something, okay? How whipped are you by Daisy?"

I started laughing. "Oh man … I don't think I'm *whipped* it's just I really care about her and want to see her happy."

Isaac nodded. "So you have feelings for her? If not necessarily in a romantic way, you still care a lot about her."

"I do. We've been friends for as long as I can remember."

"I know you have."

"But you wanna know something I've been learning? It's that sometimes not everyone is going to make it into your future."

"Yeah. People come and people go."

"Maybe Daisy is one of those cases."

"I think you're taking her not coming to prom with us to a whole new level, man."

134

"No it's not that. She's been pretty distant with us lately, you can't ignore her not coming to prom with us, and now she's not associating with us. Not to mention not really talking with me for pretty much an entire year."

"Michael, if she's moving ahead with her life, then I suggest you do the same too. You need to stop chasing after her like this. Yes you've been friends forever and you do care about her but you can't expect her to stay this way forever. She's got her life and you've got yours. She's moving on, dude."

I believe God's greatest creation was the gift of friendship. Without that, then we'd all be royally messed up.

Just then, Kimberly walked out of the ballroom, a smile on her face that stretched from ear to ear. She was sweating and panting. Her heels were off and she was holding them in her hand. She took one look at me and the smile disappeared.

"I'm going back to the bathroom," Isaac whispered to me and then took off.

She walked up to me. "Hi."

"Hey. Having fun?"

She nodded fiercely. "I just needed some air. I was looking for you! Where'd you go?"

"I, uh, I went to the bathroom and when I got back, I couldn't find you. But I saw. You were there dancing with other guys and people and whatnot."

"Oh … well yeah."

"Yeah …"

"Michael? Can I ask you something?"

"Yeah."

"When you asked me to prom, it seemed random. Like out of nowhere you asked me. Did you ask me because you wanted to go *with* me or did you just want a date to this thing?"

I sighed sharply. There were a lot of emotions I was feeling tonight.

"I asked because I thought maybe something more could come out of this for you and me," I confessed.

She stood still and kept her gaze straight at me. I felt like a fool.

"Michael …" she started. "I didn't want to lead you on. I wanted it to be clear that the only thing we can be is friends."

That felt like a punch to the gut but I knew it was true.

"You and I have become such good friends, Michael. I don't want to spoil that."

I nodded. I didn't need to say anything.

"And we both know you love Daisy. It would be wrong if I came in the middle of that. Maybe one day I could meet someone who loves me the way you love her."

"Yeah," was all I managed to say. "Sorry for thinking something more could come from this."

She smiled and then hugged me.

"Aye, why the long face?"

I breathed a laugh through my nose. *"It's been a ruff day, ya know?"*

"Ah, chin up, will ya? It's a beautiful life."

We looked each other in the eyes, she smiled and then she walked away.

I guess this is what she and Daisy had been talking about. How not everyone makes it into your future.

Isaac appeared out of the bathroom. "What happened?"

I told him.

"You know what? All this emotions and drama is too much to handle. I prefer to be a stone."

I chuckled. "Yeah. It really is."

Chapter 26

Kimberly and I didn't dance after we had that conversation in the lobby. In fact, I didn't dance at all after that. Isaac and I sat at a table away from the dancing and were talking amongst ourselves.

I tried not to think about how I hadn't even seen Daisy because of what Isaac told me. She was moving on. It was time I did too.

When prom was over, we had all agreed to get pancakes but I wasn't sure how that was all going to work out now.

"We can still go, right?" Kimberly asked me quickly.

"Yeah," I assured her. "Of course." Things were okay for us.

We figured Daisy was going out with her other friends so we left without her.

We got to the pancake house and got a table.

"Okay, what's this?" our cheery waitress asked, handing out our menus. "Why are y'all dressed up?"

"We're coming from prom," Kimberly told her with a smile.

"Oh what fun! Was it fun?"

"It was awesome!" Fabian cried. "I don't think I've ever had that much fun in my entire life!"

"Fabian, you're so loud," Isaac said in a whisper.

"Oh, *sorry!*"

She rolled her eyes and took our drink orders.

"Alright everyone," I announced. "Phones down. First one to check pays the bill."

"Bet," Isaac said, putting his down.

"Nah man that's not how it works," Kimberly said, unlocking her phone and started tapping away.

"Well, looks like Kimberly loses!" I declared.

"Yeah. Kimberly's got to pay for all the food."

"Not going to."

We ordered pancakes and we scarfed them down because dinner felt like forever ago. After pancakes, we went to a department store called Brooks that was open 24 hours. There were a few midnight shoppers there staring at us like we were the weirdest people in the world. Maybe we were.

"I need shampoo," Isaac said, heading for the cosmetics department.

"Same," Maria said.

"Are you really getting shampoo?" Fabian asked.

"Yeah," Isaac said like it was no big deal.

Isaac and Monica bought shampoo and then we were off again.

"What next?" Fabian asked, electrified.

"Next we go home and *sleep*," Kimberly stressed. "I'm tired. My feet hurt. I'm hungry. I have to go to the bathroom."

"Go inside Brooks," I said.

"Ew, no."

"Can we go to Wingman's?"

"No, Michael," Kimberly said.

I figured we were all exhausted from the night so I drove to Kimberly's house where Maria was going to spend the night. I dropped Isaac off next and then Fabian and I got to my house. We each took turns taking a shower and then I handed him a pillow and a blanket.

"Goodnight," Fabian said. He curled up into a ball and for all I knew, he was fast asleep.

I laid down on my bed and stared up at the ceiling. It was surprising what I had gone through the past few hours. But it's true what Kimberly had said.

It's a beautiful life.

Chapter 27

One Week Later

"I present to you, the class of 2015!"

Hats were thrown in the air, and the band started playing music. One by one, the rows filed out just like we had rehearsed and it was all over. We graduated. High school was over.

"HEY!" Isaac screamed once we saw each other. We barreled into each other and hugged tightly. "We did it!"

"Fabian, you slobbering walrus, come here," I said, pulling him into an embrace.

We met up with Kimberly and hugs were shared. We took pictures and it was so very emotional. I tried not to think about how some people don't make it into your future. But I wanted these people to stay with me for the rest of my life.

"Group picture!" Kimberly announced. A girl was passing by. "Hey, Sarah? Can you take a picture of us?"

Sarah took Kimberly's phone and she took a picture of the four of us. The only person missing was ...

"Hi, Michael," Daisy said once the commotion of graduation started to die down and people were going outside for more pictures.

"Hey," I said.

"We graduated."

"I know. It's crazy, isn't it? We made it."

She shook her head and smiled. "We're just about to start."

In that moment, it felt like I was talking to her for the first time in a year when it had really been two weeks.

"This isn't goodbye, is it?" I asked.

Daisy looked down and smiled again. "It might be. I'm not coming back up here."

Not even for me? I wanted to ask. But I knew she was leaving for good; ready to start her new life. Pretty soon she'd have a whole new set of friends and maybe she'd forget us. It surprised me that of all the people in my life, Daisy wouldn't be making it into my future the way I thought she would.

I looked into her eyes and saw everything about her. I saw the eight year old girl I first met. I saw the spunky eleven year old who demanded a cell phone. I saw the same girl during her "scene kid for life" phase. I saw the fourteen year old who was crying because of her mother. Then there was nothing for that year we hadn't spoken. Then there she was again

"I'm gonna miss you."

"I'll miss you too, Michael."

We hugged and the only thing I could think was how this might be the last time I'd ever hug her.

"Goodbye, Michael. Thank you for being my friend."

And then she walked away. I felt like crying. The friend I had since I was eight. The longest friendship I ever had with anyone. I wanted to cry.

"Hey, Michael?" I heard Isaac say. "You ready to go?"

"Yeah," I choked. "Let's go."

Isaac took one look at me and said, "I know you're going to miss her, but if you remember all the times you shared and know in your heart that they mean everything to you … you never really have to say goodbye."

I managed a weak smile and then I walked away from that spot. Away from Daisy. She was going to do great things with her life. It was time I should do the same.

Once I stepped outside, I looked up into the evening sky.

It was a beautiful life.

Chapter 28

Three Months Later

I was walking back to my dorm room after my last class for the day at two o' clock in a daze. I was still trying to get adjusted to how this new college schedule works. I had so much time now I wasn't sure what I should have done.

I went back to my room and put my bag on my chair. I put my hands on my lower back and stretched. I looked to my right and saw my messy roommate's side of the room. Clothes were strewn, his bed was very unkempt, and underneath his bed was the largest assortment of books, suitcases, and his shower caddy.

Daniel, clean up your side, I thought.

I flopped down on my bed and pulled out my phone. I did the usual social media browsing and saw a few pictures of Kimberly with her new college girls. I went to my photos and began looking at all the pictures I had taken during the past few months. At graduation, at the beach with all of us together. More nighttime adventures. Bonfires. Concerts. Movies. Laser tag. Bowling. Mini golf.

Sadly so far, I hadn't met the kind of friends who wanted to do any of that.

"Hey, you all wanna go bowling Friday night?"

"Oh ... no thanks ..."

"Anyone down to watch a movie?"

"A movie? Uh ... probably not."

If I was with Isaac, Fabian, Kimberly, and Daisy, they'd say yes in a heartbeat and we'd all get together and we'd go. The people I had met at Milton didn't seem like they wanted to do much of anything. I was trying my best to make new friends. It felt like I was in first grade all over again trying to make new friends.

Seeing their faces and remembering all of our times together brought back bittersweet memories.

I saw a picture of us at a pier and I remembered how a homeless man came up to Isaac and thought he was his long lost brother and tried to convince him he was.

The next picture was a candid shot of Kimberly at the beach and her eyes were looking up but they were cross eyed. I laughed out loud by myself.

And then I thought about the night Daisy and I ran off together and how we went to Lake Geneva and jumped in the water together. And every moment after.

Then the memories of the one girl that meant everything to me rushed back like a flash flood. All the times we spent laughing, talking, spending time together. It was a close relationship with a deep understanding of the other person. We were comfortable together. We were partners in crime and I was mad for her. I learned that being alone isn't so bad. It's being forgotten by someone you will *never* forget.

Isaac and I talked but since we were so far away from each other, we didn't talk as much as I might have hoped. Kimberly and I started to fall off once August hit and she started getting things ready for her school. Fabian and I didn't talk much anymore either.

It made me depressed to experience first-hand once vibrant friendships slowly fade away.

I sat up from my bed and went to my phonebook and stopped myself at Daisy's name. It was so easy to call her and hear her voice. Suddenly there wasn't anything in the world I wanted to do more than talk to her.

I got up from my bed, grabbed my backpack and my windbreaker. I grabbed a water bottle from my fridge and stuffed it in my bag. I made sure I had my phone, keys, and wallet. I saw I had about five dollars in cash. *Poor college kid.*

I walked out of my room and left the hall. I kept on walking until I got to the parking garage where I got inside Becky.

At least Becky is still here with me.

I turned it on and drove out of the garage and down the street and eventually got on the highway where I kept on driving.

By the time I got to Rockford, it was six o' clock. Traffic was a nightmare.

My legs were wobbly as I parked in one of the Rockford University parking lots. I wasn't even sure where Daisy was. It was evening, she probably was back in her apartment. And it wasn't like I knew where that was.

What was I doing? I'm definitely out of my mind

I walked around their campus, hoping to see a glimpse of Daisy. It was a fairly small campus. I started to think this was the wrong idea when I heard her voice. I looked and saw a group of people walking out of a building.

146

There were five girls and two guys. My heart started beating rapidly and I was feeling so nervous.

"Daisy?" I said.

I'm definitely *out of my mind.*

Her group stopped walking and looked at me, confused. I didn't blame them. I was a stranger coming up to them.

"Michael?" she asked.

She came into view and she looked so much different than when I last saw her. Her skin looked a little darker from what I remembered. Her hair, still brown, was longer and fell straight down her shoulders. Something about her eyes seemed different to me. She didn't look tired and *stuck* as she once described herself. She looked free. She looked beautiful. Or maybe she always looked like this but since I hadn't seen her in a long time, it was new to me. Her sad eyes were replaced with a new life in a beautiful place.

"Um, what are you doing here?" she asked. She almost looked worried.

"I came to see you," I told her.

"Daisy, who is this?" one of the girls in her group asked.

"Um ..."

She was hesitating?

"He's an old friend from back home." Now her friends were looking at me like I was so weird. Which, let's face it, I was at the moment. "You guys go ahead, I'll catch up with you."

Her friends skulked away, still wondering who I am and why I randomly showed up at her school.

"Michael …" she started. "What are you doing here? Did you drive all the way down here?"

I couldn't believe what I was doing.

"Yeah."

She sighed and I wasn't sure what kind of sigh it was. Frustration? There was a time when I could automatically tell how she was by the way she looked. But now it was like looking at a stranger. All over again.

"What's going on, Michael? Why are you here?"

"I came here to thank you for being my friend all these years. I just wanted you to know that."

She looked at me like I was crazy. But I didn't care. I came here to tell her that because I needed her to know.

"Yeah."

"Wait. Hold on. Michael. Are you alone?"

"Yeah."

She swallowed a lump in her throat. I couldn't get over how beautiful she looked.

"Are you hungry? I can get you a meal swipe if you want."

I shook my head. "No it's okay. Really. I just wanted to tell you that."

She pursed her lips and gave me a look. It was a look of pity.

"Michael, I know we've been great friends all our lives but remember what I told you that night? Not everyone in your present makes it to your future. This is one of those times."

I felt the air go out of me.

"You don't love me, Michael. We're friends and that's all we can ever be. I'm sorry."

Each word was like a punch to the gut but I stood there and took it.

"Please don't bring up my past, Michael. I came here to forget it. I don't want to remember it."

"Does that mean I'm part of your past?"

Her expression changed to a solemn one. I was just *waiting* for her to say something that would break my already broken heart.

"You're not a part of my past in *that* sense. All it means is that right now, we're on different paths."

I wanted to say so much more. I had so many more questions about us. If our friendship was still alive or was I just torturing myself.

"You're going to meet an amazing girl one day, Michael. I'm just not her. Don't let this stop you from achieving all of the amazing things you're meant to do."

That was something I told her oh so long ago. At that moment, it seemed like the times we shared were slipping away. Falling off a cliff.

Who's going to be there for me when my heartstrings come undone? I wanted to ask her. *I thought we were sleep-walkers.*

"Okay," I said dumbly. "Okay …"

"It's gonna be okay, Michael."

I swallowed a basketball in my throat.

"Goodbye."

And then I watched her walk out of my life for a second time.

I drove back to Milton University, walked into my room, shut the door and ran my hands through my hair. Had I just screwed up the best friendship I ever had? What was I *thinking?*

Homework was the last thing on my mind at that point. So I changed clothes and got under my covers and tried hard to go to sleep. Of course the conversation was playing over and over in my head in addition to everything we had been through.

Eventually my numerous thoughts lulled to sleep. When I woke up the next morning, I saw a text from Isaac from the night before.

Hey, wanna hang out this weekend?

About the Author:

AJAY JOSEPH began writing stories when he was six years old. His passion for books and reading continued well into his high school days where he wrote several of his works for young adults. A recurring theme in his books is a message of faith, hope, and love. It is because Ajay personally believes these three attributes are stronger than doubt, fear, and hate.

He lives in Chicago.